"Like Lansdale on meth, or '80s action-movie icon Shane Black on crack, I have yet to read anything by Howe that didn't have me laughing so hard I wondered more than once if I might have sprained something vital inside of me. He's done it again with *Tijuana Donkey Showdown*. The only thing I hate about this guy's books is the fact that, as soon as I finish one, there's not another I can start right away. Dammit." —James Newman, author of *Ugly As Sin, Odd Man Out*, and *Animosity*

"Adam Howe has oodles of insane talent. *Tijuana Donkey Showdown* reads like the script of the greatest B-movie ever, written by the unholy offspring of Joe R. Lansdale and Jeff Strand, and directed by Uwe Boll. Howe is a purveyor of beautiful, ridiculous violence, and I hope the misadventures of Reggie Levine continue for a long time." —Pete Kahle, award-winning author of *The Specimen*

"Adam Howe's latest offering rips along at the speed of sound, delivering action-packed thrills, uncountable surprises—both light and dark—and edgy, trademark humor, all of it rendered in such vivid prose it practically shimmers on the page. Another winner from an emerging master." —Sean Costello, author of *Squall* and *Finders Keepers*

"Adam Howe is one of the funniest, sickest, most insane writers working today. The man has no filter!" —Jeff Strand, author of *Dead Clown Barbeque*

"Adam Howe sports neither Burt Reynolds' mustache or Steven Seagal's ponytail. He's a beat poet of lowbrow Americana, but also a British dude. And just when you think there couldn't possibly be any more surprises, he drops another book to show you how wrong you are. One of the absolute best writers working today." —Adam Cesare, *The Con Season* and *Tribesmen*

"Adam Howe's *Tijuana Donkey Showdown* is funny and vicious, a lunatic noir carnival ride that gleefully drags you through the muck and will make you thank him for it. Fans of Mickey Spillane and L. A. Morse will rejoice and demand more of Howe's scoundrel antihero Reggie Levine. How a Brit has any business writing down and dirty Americana this well is a mystery to me, but he's got the goods and the goods are goddamned hilarious." —Ed Kurtz, author of *The Rib From Which I Remake the World*

"Adam Howe's work forces you to laugh and cringe the way you could previously only do while watching a one-armed drunk trying to juggle revved-up chainsaws, and *Tijuana Donkey Showdown* is his best book yet. Fast, filthy, the violent literary equivalent of a Nic Cage lovechild who grew up watching 80s action movies in the back of a stinky roadside attraction." —Gabino Iglesias, author of *Zero Saints*

"Adam Howe is a fearless writer with an unfettered imagination, and with *Tijuana Donkey Showdown*, he takes the reader on a ride that starts fast and crazy and only revs up from there. He's lurid and elegant, trashy and witty, a literary provocateur who disturbs and entertains in equal measure." —Scott Adlerberg, author of *Graveyard Love*

"Adam Howe is probably the best writer I've discovered in years, and I do nothing with my spare time but read and write, which should tell you something. *Tijuana Donkey Showdown* is not only his funniest work to date. It might also be his best." —Joseph Hirsch, author of *Kentucky Bestiary* and *Flash Blood*

OTHER WORKS BY ADAM HOWE

Die Dog or Eat the Hatchet

Includes the Novellas:

Damn Dirty Apes
Die Dog or Eat the Hatchet
Gator Bait

Black Cat Mojo

Includes the Novellas:

Of Badgers & Porn Dwarfs
Jesus in a Dog's Ass
Frank, The Snake, & The Snake

Plus Bonus Short:
The Mad Butcher of Plainfield's Chariot of Death

**Read the first Reggie
Levine misadventure,
Damn Dirty Apes, in
the *Die Dog or Eat the
Hatchet* collection,
available at Amazon and
other online retailers.**

Washed-up prizefighter Reggie Levine is eking a living as a strip club bouncer when he's offered an unlikely shot at redemption. The Bigelow Skunk Ape—a mythical creature said to haunt the local woods—has kidnapped the high school football mascot, Boogaloo Baboon. Now it's up to Reggie to lead a misfit posse including a plucky stripper, the town drunk, and legend-in-his-own-mind skunk ape hunter Jameson T. Salisbury. Their mission: Slay the beast and rescue their friend. But not everything is as it seems, and as our heroes venture deeper into the heart of darkness, they will discover worse things waiting in the woods than just the Bigelow Skunk Ape. The story the Society for the Preservation of the North American Skunk Ape tried to ban; *Damn Dirty Apes* mixes *Roadhouse* with *Jaws* with *Sons of Anarchy*, to create a rollicking romp of 80s-style action/adventure, creature horror and pitch-black comedy.

First Comet Press Trade Paperback Edition
December 2016

Tijuana Donkey Showdown copyright © 2016
by Adam Howe
All Rights Reserved.

"Clean-up On Aisle 3" was first published in *Thuglit 19*
(August 2015)

Cover illustration and poster art by Mike Tenebrae
tenebraestudios.net

ISBN 13: 978-1-936964-03-1

Visit Comet Press on the web at:
www.cometpress.us
facebook.com/cometpress
twitter.com/cometpress

WWW.COMETPRESS.US

AUTHOR'S DISCLAIMER

While writing this book, I discovered I was going to be a father for the first time. (My daughter, Georgia Mae Howe, was born on the 24th July 2016.) On learning the news, chief among the whirlwind of emotions I felt was abject shame, and stark terror that my child might one day read the filth I write.

My first impulse was to destroy the manuscript, much as Mrs. Robert Louis Stevenson threw her husband's first draft of *Jekyll & Hyde* into the fire.

Sadly, I was already under contract to Comet Press to deliver the book. On the advice of my lawyer, who has yet to forgive me for the controversy caused by my previous novella, *Damn Dirty Apes,* and the ensuing legal battle with the Society for the Preservation of the North American Skunk Ape, I honored the contract with grudging good grace.

The contract expires in four years, after which I intend to withdraw the book from publication; I only pray my daughter will not have learned to read by then, and will make every effort to stunt her development to ensure that this doesn't happen.

I hereby renounce this work, and would urge you not read it. *Tijuana Donkey Showdown* will be the last of my peculiar brand of gutter pulp. I will henceforth write only literary works, navel-gazing fluff detailing the valiant first-world travails of a thirty-something Caucasian male writer, and new father, as he struggles to maintain the perfect work/life balance without sacrificing his artistic integrity, and his responsibilities as a scribe for the common man.

So, I hope you enjoyed the degeneracy while it lasted, folks. There will be no more porn dwarfs, or diarrheic Jack Russell terriers; no more man-eating giant snakes, gators, or oversexed orangutans; no more scenes involving deranged rednecks fisting victims with disembodied limbs, or torture-by-rat.

It's over . . .

I'm just fucking around.

The kid changes nothing.

I hope you dig *Tijuana Donkey Showdown*; I had a lotta fun writing it.

Depending on the reader response, I may write a third Reggie Levine misadventure. Given the hell I put the poor bastard through, I don't think he could feasibly survive beyond three stories. I've got a killer set-up for a third book, but it's all for shit if no one wants to read it, so drop me a line and let me know at Facebook, Goodreads, and Twitter @Adam_G_Howe . . .

Although, hell, I might write it anyway, just to spite ya'll.

And please take the time to leave an Amazon review, ideally full of gushing praise, but I'll settle for rabid hate. Amazon reviews are about the best gift you can give an indie writer, and help us more than you probably realize.

Until next time . . .

Farewell and adieu,
Adam Howe

CONTENTS

FOREWORD
BY JAMES NEWMAN

I really want to hate Adam Howe.

It's a good thing there are 4,000 miles between us and most of it is ocean. 'Cause I'd like nothing more than to punch him in the face.

Allow me to explain.

My disdain for Adam Howe isn't because he's a bigger film geek than I am. I like to think I know a lot about horror/cult cinema (you don't write a book called 666 HAIR-RAISING HORROR MOVIE TRIVIA QUESTIONS, after all, unless you know what you're talking about). But chewing the fat with Adam for any length of time always makes me feel inadequate. Like we just whipped out our dicks to see whose was most impressive and he had five or six inches on me plus the girth to go with it. In our conversations Adam and I constantly quote lines from our favorite movies, back and forth, rapid-fire, like Quentin Tarantino hopped up on birthday cake and bathtub crank. But at some point, it never fails . . . there's always a moment when our nerd-chatter comes to a screeching halt, when I'm forced to admit about some movie he just mentioned, "I, uh, can't say I'm familiar with that one. Guess I need to look it up."

Adam doesn't gloat when this happens. Much. It doesn't chap my hide any less.

But there's a lot more to it than that . . .

I don't despise Adam Howe due to the fact that, even though he's British, after reading the guy's prose for the first time I was fully convinced that he's Southern just like me. I was sure he lived just down the road—you know, "over yonder" by the "crick" out past what the old folks still call "colored town." Read his work and you'll see what I mean. At first, you're likely to think Adam was born somewhere deep in the heart of Texas. His writing voice has a Southern drawl so thick it makes the great Joe R. Lansdale sound like he grew up on the south side of Brooklyn. It makes my own *Ugly As Sin*, a tale of "white trash noir" set in the Blue Ridge Mountains of North Carolina, read like a cozy mystery about a Scottish sleuth sipping tea with his pinkie sticking straight up in the air.

That ain't fair. It ain't fair at all that Adam writes like he was born and raised south of the Mason-Dixon line. He's not even FROM here!

Still, not-so-thinly-veiled xenophobia aside, that's not why I want to hate Adam Howe.

Hard as it might be for you to believe this, I don't even want to inflict bodily harm upon Adam because his short story "Jumper" won a contest a few years ago, a contest judged by none other than STEPHEN KING. I can imagine his smug face (not Mr. King's, I've got nothing against him, except for encouraging this asshole early on) as he boarded that plane to fly across the big pond and have dinner with a living legend. Supposedly they talked about all kinds of cool stuff, long into the night, like old friends. At one point I hear they discussed RETURN OF THE LIVING DEAD, one of my all-time favorite movies. That shit fills me with so much envy I'm worried I might break out in hives every time I think about it. So I don't. I don't think about it.

But, again, Adam's man-date with the Master of Horror isn't the reason I want to hate him.

No . . . I'll tell you the #1 reason I want to hate this fucker.

It's because he's so damn GOOD. And he just keeps getting better.

Adam began his career as an aspiring screen-writer before turning his attention to prose (what I wouldn't give to see THOSE movies!). To date, he has a handful of published short stories and two novella collections to his name (if you haven't already, go buy *Die Dog Or Eat the Hatchet* and *Black Cat Mojo* as soon as you finish reading this . . . I promise you'll thank me later). Now, that's not exactly a vast body of prose, a testament to a craft honed to perfection after decades of hard work. Yet you'd think the guy's been writing for the last 30 or 40 years. He's got the skills of a seasoned pro, lemme tell ya.

He makes this look EASY. His work is so confi-dent, so tight, so . . . UNPUTDOWNABLE (I'm well aware that's not a word, but leave it to some hotshot writer like Howe if he thinks he can come up with something better; I'm not even getting paid to write this shit).

That, my friends, is the sign of an artist who's gonna be around for a long time. He's making his mark like a bad rash on your nether-regions after a night with a dirty woman. He's here to stay, and good luck finding the right antibiotic to make him go away. Like I said in my blurb for the book you hold in your hands: the only thing I hate about his work is the fact that there's not more of it out there. I finish one thing by Adam, I'm immediately ready to start another.

And that's why I wanna grab Adam Howe by the throat and give him an old-fashioned ass-whoopin', Southern-style. Show that Limey bastard how we do it over here in 'Murica. I wanna do it in front of his wife and kid. And when I'm done knocking his dick in the dirt I want to spit that PERFECT one-liner in his face just to add insult to injury, a line from some kick-ass cult flick Adam has never seen and he never will 'cause—haha—it's banned in his country. Or something.

My guess is, after reading *Tijuana Donkey Show-down,* you'll feel the same way. Especially if you're a writer too. 'Cause like I said . . . it ain't fair that he's so good.

I guess that's enough ranting for now. I'm past my allotted word count and I've got work to do . . .

Oh, I didn't mention that I'm collaborating on a novel with one of my favorite writers?

I won't tell you who it is. But you know what they say: If you can't beat 'em, join 'em.

The face-punching will have to wait, I suppose. At least until we are done.

James Newman
October 12, 2016

TIJUANA DONKEY SHOWDOWN

"When people tell me something's over the top, I say, 'Well, you tell me where the top is, and I'll tell you whether I'm over it.'"

—Nicolas Cage

"If I appeal to anyone, I hope it's the man who picks up the garbage."

—Lee Marvin

"This is a respectable gentlemen's club, not some damn Tijuana donkey show!"

—Walton Wiley, proprietor of
The Henhouse, *Damn Dirty Apes*

ONE

FOR A GREAT BUICK
CALL 555-7617

1.

I first met Harry Muffet in the men's room at The Henhouse, Walt Wiley's titty tonk in Bigelow town, where some fella, looked like an Orc from a *Lord of the Rings* movie, only not as pretty, was using Harry's head as a toilet plunger.

The Orc had Harry by the ankles, dunking him headfirst into the crapper like he was dipping a donut in his morning cup of Joe. He dragged Harry's head from the bowl and granted him a gulp of air to prolong his misery. The Orc clearly hadn't done him the courtesy of flushing the commode. Harry's face was freckled with the previous occupant's leavings, maybe the Orc's, in which case this was a premeditated deal. Filth was spewing up over the rim of the bowl, spreading across the cracked tile floor of the men's room. I shook my head and sighed, not needing three guesses to know who'd be cleaning up the mess. This was already shaping up to be a regular rare morning. The men's room door clattered shut behind me. The Orc's head cranked around, and he glared at me, a tree stump of a man with a patchy red beard, like even his facial fuzz wanted off his ugly mug. He wore a sweat-stained shirt with a trucking company logo on the back, and his name was stitched across the breast, maybe so he wouldn't forget it. That name was OTIS. Well, of course it was. In my experience, you can't reason with an Otis. They're ornery as hell.

I stayed standing where I was at the entrance to the john, my new copy of *Ring* magazine tucked under my arm, and last night's microwave burrito, which had seemed like a swell idea at the time, bolting through my bowels like a fugitive fleeing for the border. I fidgeted from foot to foot. "You fellas gonna be long?" Because the men's room at The Henhouse had just the one commode, not counting the sink, although on rowdy weekends, a lot of fellas did count it.

Harry came up for air and spluttered, "The hell you think's going on here?"

"I wouldn't want to jump to conclusions."

"Do I look like a willing participant in this?"

On consideration, I had to admit he didn't.

"And you work here, right?"

I glanced down at the black tee shirt I was wearing. STAFF was printed across the chest, except most of the 'A' had rubbed off in the wash, so it looked more like it read STIFF. My boss, Walt Wiley (for my sins, he was also my best friend) thought that was hysterical and refused to spring for a new shirt.

I looked back at Harry and nodded reluctantly.

"So do something!"

Otis glanced between Harry and me. "This piece-a shit a friend of yours?"

Harry started telling him how we were lifelong buddies, willing to *die* for each other—

Unable to hear over Harry's yammering, Otis shoved his head back down into the toilet bowl. Harry's gargling cries echoed through the men's room.

"Nope," I said to Otis. "But I *am* the head bouncer here . . ." I couldn't resist using the trumped-up job title Walt had given me instead of a raise.

Except Otis called me on it. "There's *other* bouncers in this dive?"

"The point is," I said, "I can't allow you to drown a man in our commode." Not least because I was likely to contaminate the crime scene when I took a dump in it directly afterwards.

Otis's face crumpled in disappointment. Like he couldn't believe what this country was coming to. That a man was no longer free to drown someone in a strip club toilet. *Thanks, Obama.* "You don't understand, mister. This hornswoggling sonofabitch sold my sister a deathtrap on wheels. He damn near killed her!"

Harry came up for air and protested, "I can't be held responsible once the car leaves the lot!"

"She wasn't fifty yards off the lot when the brakes failed," Otis said. "She nearly went under a truck!"

"Well . . ." Harry said, with a sheepish chuckle. "Shit happens."

Which was an unfortunate choice of words, because down he went again.

The next time Otis let Harry up for air, I canted my head like an art critic and took a closer look at him, and I suddenly recognized his face, soiled though it was, from the advertising billboards around town. The signs said:

HARRY'S PRE-OWNED AMERICAN AUTO
Buying a NEW pre-owned?
You'll be happy as Larry you bought from Harry!

In the billboards, Harry was holding up a set of car keys, grinning like a fisherman with the catch of the day. Behind him was a fleet of gleaming luxury cars that looked nothing like the decrepit beaters I saw on display whenever I passed his dealership. He was wearing the used-car salesman's uniform of a check sports jacket and slacks, with a Stars and Stripes tie. He boasted a magnificent bouffant of hair, and a mustache like Tom Selleck's in *Magnum*, if Magnum lost his private eye license due to conduct unbecoming and went to hell in a bourbon bottle.

Given the ubiquity of the billboards around town, and the late night TV commercials that aired on local cable, Harry Muffet was something like a celebrity in Bigelow. I made the mistake of saying, "Hey, I know you."

Harry clutched at my words like a drowning man clinging to flotsam.

"That's right, Reggie! You do! Of course you do! Help me, please!"

I wasn't overly surprised that Harry knew my name; I was something like a local celebrity myself. Even Otis narrowed his eyes, sized me up and down. "Reggie Levine?"

Once upon a time, I was a prizefighter. I coulda been a contender . . . Until the day I fought Boar Hog Brannon for the light heavyweight state title, and he damn near beat me to death. (Years later, when it was of scant consolation, I discovered he'd cheated in our match . . . but that's another story.) More recently, and memorably, my claim to fame was what most folks in town called the 'skunk ape thing.' A couple of years ago, a creature believed to be the mythical Bigelow Skunk Ape—a backwoods Bigfoot with B.O.—abducted our high school football mascot, Boogaloo Baboon, plus the man inside the monkey suit, Ned Pratt. I found myself among the posse who set off into the Sticks on a rescue mission—along with Eliza Tuttle, who used to dance topless at The Henhouse, and who now acts, often topless, in Hollywood B-pictures; Eliza's boyfriend, the late Lester Swash; and self-proclaimed skunk ape hunter Jameson T. Salisbury. Now it turned out the skunk ape wasn't no skunk ape; it was *just* a big-ass orangutan called Mofo. Unfortunately for us, Mofo was bad-tempered, and randy as a goat with two peckers—poor Ned bore the brunt of his lust. To make matters worse, Mofo was also a member of the Damn Dirty Apes motorcycle club. The Apes were cooking crystal meth out at Herb Planter's old hog farm, and were not best pleased when we stumbled across their operation. Needless to say, things went FUBAR right quick. Eliza, Ned and me were lucky to escape with our lives. Salisbury and Lester weren't so fortunate.

Probably that sounds a little strange to you?

Well, no shit. I was there and I *still* struggle to believe it really happened.

Maybe you saw the Hollywood movie they made? *Damn Dirty Apes.* Swept the board at the Razzies last year. Eliza debuted as herself in the movie and did a pretty fair job of it. Me, I've got a mug that'd break a radio. Nicolas Cage played yours truly, sporting a mullet that made his *Con Air*-'do seem conservative, even though I haven't styled my hair like that since the nineties. But who the hell am I to argue with the artistic choices of Nicolas Cage? The Man's an icon.

Ever since the movie was released, people had started visiting The Henhouse to hear me tell the story in person, or to ask me questions about Nicolas Cage, who I never met, so they'd always leave grumbling and disappointed. Stranger still were the folks who started bringing me their problems to solve, like I was some kinda one-man *A-Team* who could help them. But worst of all were the scalp-hunters; the badasses who wanted to test their mettle by dancing a few rounds with the Skunk Ape Slayer, Reggie Levine.

It looked like Otis was the latest of these knuckleheads.

Just bigger and uglier than usual.

He stomped from the toilet stall like a troll from

his cave. He was still clutching Harry by the ankle. One handed, no less. A show of brute strength that hardly filled me with joy at the prospect of going toe to toe with him.

"I heard-a you," Otis sneered, "Mr. *so-called* Skunk Ape Slayer."

With a grunt, he flung Harry clear the length of the men's room. If used-car salesman tossing was an Olympic event, Otis would've been a gold medalist.

Harry crashed against the condom dispenser and thudded to the floor. A rain of rubbers ejaculated from the machine. Novelty rubbers, I should add, because for most of the patrons at The Henhouse, getting laid was indeed a novelty. "We're selling fantasy here," Walt liked to say.

Otis marched towards me, chinking his neck and balling ham-hock fists.

"I'd like to see you beat on me like you beat on that orangutan," he said.

Did I mention that those Damn Dirty Apes made me box Mofo the orangutan? True story.

"I don't want no trouble here," I said, "all I want is a crap."

Otis loosened my bowels with a left hook to the gut and I filled my shorts with liquidized burrito. I managed to wheeze, "Goddamn it—" Then he grabbed the front of my shirt and hoisted me up into the air. The top of my skull cracked the ceiling light with a crunch of plastic. The light bulb started spazzing, turning the men's room into the world's seediest discotheque. Still clutching my copy of *Ring* magazine, I swatted Otis over the head with it, like I was trying to housebreak a puppy. That didn't do much else except piss him off—so I jabbed him in the eye with the rolled-up end—now he was *really* mad. He let out a roar and pitched me across the room, like he was trying to beat the record he'd set hurling Harry. I crashed through the flimsy wooden wall of the toilet stall, reducing years of historic graffiti to kindling.

On hands and knees inside the buckled stall, I clutched the crapper and tried to steady myself. But before I could clamber to my feet, Otis landed on my back like Hulk Hogan leaping down from the turnbuckle. The breath woofed from my lungs. Otis gripped me by the hair and started shoving my head down towards the shit-choked toilet bowl.

Snatching the porcelain lid from the toilet top, I swung the slab back over my shoulder, and smashed the heavy tablet in two across Otis's forehead. Otis let out a grunt. His hands relaxed on the back of my neck. Squirming free from his grip, I scrambled across the stall away from him, wedging myself between the commode and the wall, like someone seeking shelter during an earthquake. Otis was out on his feet, teetering ominously. His eyeballs rolled up white in his skull. Blood streamed from the gash in his forehead where I'd brained him with the cistern slab. He dropped to one knee like he was about to propose. Then, instead of popping the question, he toppled forwards, his bulk crashing down on the toilet bowl and shattering the porcelain to rubble. A tsunami of sewage flooded across the floor, drenching me in a stinking spray of brown-and-yellow filth.

But, thank God, at least Otis was done for.

I glanced across the men's room, expecting to see Harry cowering beneath the condom dispenser, grateful for me having saved his life. But he was gone. The sneaky sonofabitch must have vamoosed while I was tussling with Otis.

I leaned against the wall and caught my breath, not to mention a ferocious whiff of ripe human waste. Otis was splayed facedown in a lake of piss. I didn't have the heart to just leave him to drown, so I rolled him onto his back. Okay: So I kicked him onto his back. *Hard*. He deserved that much.

Surveying the flooded floor, I spotted a leather wallet propped up against a turd. It must've fallen from Harry's pocket while Otis was shaking him upside down. The wallet, I mean, not the turd. I fetched the wallet from the floor and tossed it in the sink and ran the faucet to clean it some. I'd return it to its owner with a few choice words. My new *Ring* magazine was beyond salvage, reduced to mulch, and that really pissed me off, because I had to order it special from the store in town and there was no telling how long I'd be waiting for a replacement.

I grabbed Otis by his ankles and started yoking him from the men's room.

2.

The Henhouse was much as I'd left it when I went to take a crap.

In fact, the place had hardly changed in the couple years since the skunk ape thing.

Same slab of oak bar, fringed with old Christmas lights; same shrine of dusty liquor bottles behind it. Same butcher-block tables and chairs, same shadowy booths with slashed-vinyl seats. Same old Lou; huddled at the end of the runway stage like a seedy off-Broadway theater director, tithing the dancing gals from his pile of palm-clammy singles. Same old Marlene, The Henhouse's sumo-sized dancing queen, working the stage in her G-string and pasties, spinning her tassels like Chinook rotor blades. Same cigarette-scarred pool table. Same *Smokey and the Bandit* pinball machine; I'd lost my high score to another pinball wizard but was determined to claw it back, no matter how many quarters it cost me. The old rotary phone in the telephone kiosk had been repaired, but cell phones had been invented during the time it was out of service.

Walt Wiley, the owner of The Henhouse, was holding court behind the bar. "Mark my words," he proclaimed, "when the cops catch this Backseat Strangler sonofabitch, he'll be a Mexican—" The usual barflies were lining the oak slab like crows along a telephone wire, hanging on Walt's every word in the forlorn hope of a free shot.

On the wall behind the bar was the framed, yellowing news cutting commemorating my fight with Boar Hog Brannon:

BIGELOW BOY BRUTALIZED IN PRIZEFIGHT

Walt had since added more news cuttings about the skunk ape thing—for the tourists, he claimed—plus the postcards we'd occasionally receive from Eliza out in Hollywood.

There was even a framed poster from the *Damn Dirty Apes* movie.

It was signed in a shaky hand:

To my good friend, Walt

Nick

Walt had, of course, signed the poster himself— which was why Nic Cage had misspelled his name— and then sworn me to secrecy.

Other than that, yep, same old Henhouse, all right.

And same old Reggie Levine, neck-deep in shit, only literally this time.

3.

I ankle-dragged Otis from the men's room, smearing sewage across the floor in our wake as I lugged him to the door. Walt took one look at me, and he must've remembered the funniest joke he ever heard, because he started slapping the bar slab and laughing his ass off.

"Toilet humor," he said. "Can't beat it."

He said to the barflies, "Take a pitcher on your phone, would you, someone?"

Great, I thought. A new addition to my Wall of Shame.

"Go take a look at the men's room," I said to Walt, "let's see how you like toilet humor then."

I dragged Otis outside, left him in the parking lot to wake up and hobble home. He could count himself lucky I didn't call our local lawman, Constable Randy-Ray Gooch. Although frankly, the fewer people saw me looking like this, the better.

I went back inside, dripping on the WIPE YOUR FEET welcome mat. Walt was still snickering. "You see a used-car salesman go running past?" I asked him. "Covered in shit? Guilty look on his face for leaving me to get killed?"

Walt considered a moment. "Apart from the guilty look, you must mean Harry Muffet."

"Walt," I said, "I'm gonna need to take a personal day."

"You asking or telling me?"

"You really want me working, looking and smelling like this?"

I could tell he was tempted to keep me around, if only to bust my chops. But in the end the stench won out. "See you bright n' early tomorrow, Champ."

Before I could leave, he called out: "Reggie, wait!"

I turned back around and was blinded by a camera flash. When my vision returned, Walt was grinning at the photo he'd taken on a camera phone.

"Oh yeah," he said, "that's a keeper."

4.

I fetched a sheet of tarp from the bed of my truck, spread it across the seats like a dog blanket, and then

I drove home to change with the windows wide open and my head hanging out like Rover on a road trip.

With the money I got for the movie rights to my story—not as much as you might think—I'd put a deposit on a nice little house in a goodish part of town. Figured I'd been living in my crummy apartment above the thrift store long enough. I also treated myself to the new secondhand Ford, thankfully from one of Harry Muffet's competitors, so it still ran. The rest of the money I'd given to Walt to invest on my behalf, if only to stop him nagging me. Walt fancied himself as Bigelow's answer to Donald Trump—and politically speaking, he wasn't far wrong. Walt had talked a great game about how he was going to turn my little nest egg into a fortune. But it turned out that's all it was: Talk. He promptly lost the lot to a Nigerian phishing scam. So, thanks to Walt, I lost all my movie money and forfeited the deposit I'd put on the house. A nice young couple lives there now. They've just had their first child, a little boy. Sometimes I'll drive past the place—not in a creepy way, I hope—and wonder what might've been . . .

Long story short: I was still living in the same old flophouse above the thrift store.

I parked in the spot outside the thrift store that the owner Mrs. Gowran reserved for me. Mrs. Gowran was a kindhearted bird whose innate need to mother matched my own to be mothered; we got along swell. She'd put aside for me the men's adventure novels people donated to the store, as well as any hand-me-down duds she thought might flatter me more than my regular *white trash chic* wardrobe. All she asked in return was I occasionally help out in the store with any heavy lifting, which these days, was as close to a workout as I got.

For some time now Mrs. Gowran had been threatening to set me up with her niece from Ayresville—which was a dubious proposition. See, I'd already met her nephew, and not to be unkind, but if his sister looked like him, the gal was likely to be less an oil painting, than Neanderthal cave art.

Now you could make a solid argument I had no right being picky; I've got a mug you wouldn't wish on a warthog. But the truth of the matter was that my heart belonged to another. She didn't want it, of course—and sometimes I'd wonder if Cupid's aim was off, considering how unobtainable the objects of my affection were—but it was hers all the same.

Shelby Boon was the new town veterinarian. She'd taken over the practice from Edgar Dubrow, after the *Bigelow Bugle* exposed Dubrow's involvement in a neo-Nazi dogfighting racket, and he was struck off the veterinary register.

Shelby had the kind of big brown eyes Van Morrison must've been singing about, a tomboyish crop of raven-black hair, and cute little dimples in her cheeks and chin. Nor had it escaped my attention that there was one humdinger of a body beneath the practical shirt and pants she wore. Coming from a guy who works in a strip club there's no higher compliment, as I told her when we first met. It would be an understatement to say Shelby was unimpressed by that comment; or the rumors I had killed, not just an orangutan, but also a bear cub.

As I climbed from the truck, caked in human filth and reeking of ditto, with the sheet of shitty tarpaulin glued to the seat of my pants like an errant scrap of toilet paper, Shelby emerged from the thrift store, where she'd been checking up on Mrs. Gowran's cat, Bootsy, after his recent operation.

Shelby saw me and stopped in her tracks. I froze, hoping maybe if I didn't move she wouldn't see me, like a T-Rex. Then the wind changed direction, she made a kind of gagging noise, and I knew the game was up.

I raked my hand through my hair in a futile effort to make myself look presentable. "Morning, Doc." Powdered excrement flaked like brown dandruff from my crap-caked locks.

Shelby shuddered in disgust.

Inside the store, I caught Mrs. Gowran shaking her head in despair; I guessed I'd probably blown it with her niece now, too.

"Long story," I said to Shelby.

"I don't want to hear it," she said, backing away from me.

"Gotcha." Feeling like I'd been kicked in the heart, I squelched past her to the outside stairs leading up to my flophouse.

5.

You're expecting the Ritz, right? Sorry to disappoint you. Unless you envisioned a Ritz cracker box, in which case, yeah, the place was about that size. It was a combination living/bedroom/kitchen kinda deal, with an en-suite bathroom. Kinda one big room, really. Only not so big. But I'd made it my own and decorated the place with empty takeout cartons and crushed beer cans and packratted piles of pulp books and *Ring* magazine back issues. A withered brown cactus plant clung to life on the windowsill. Above the unmade sofa bed was the poster from *Rocky* you'll find on the wall of every boxer's crib.

I fetched a brewski from the icebox, glugging it down as I showered the shit off me, but I couldn't sluice away Shelby's look of disgust.

Face it, Levine. You're just a broke-down strip club palooka, living in a shoebox above a thrift store. A classy broad like Shelby Boon would never look twice at a pug like you. Hell, you'd be lucky to land a date with Lorena Bobbitt.

The shame of it was that I'd actually *had* a second chance to get my shit together and make something of myself. Instead I'd let the opportunity slip through my fingers. Sure, after the skunk ape thing, and the money from the movie, I'd made a half-assed attempt to better myself. I'd put that deposit on the house. Even made some enquiries about opening my own boxing gym, thinking maybe I could help disadvantaged kids—which in Bigelow was most every kid in town—help 'em stay out of trouble by beating hell out of each other. But it was all just a pipedream. No different than Walt kidding himself (at my expense) that he was a Wall Street whiz. In the end I'd been content just to sit on my ass at The Henhouse, pissing away my fifteen minutes of fame until all I was left with were the familiar regrets and self-loathing. I couldn't shake the feeling that by giving Walt my money to invest I'd subconsciously sabotaged myself. What the hell was wrong with me; did I just fear change?

I showered for about an hour. Avoided my reflection in the medicine cabinet mirror as I cinched a towel around my spare tire. Fetched another cold one from the icebox. Then I went and slumped on the sofa bed, gazing up at that poster of Rocky and Adrian. *Was it really too much to ask?*

Hearing faint ticking, I glanced at my watch on the upturned orange crate that served as my side table. The watch had been a gift from Nicolas Cage, thanking me for my contribution to the *Damn Dirty Apes* movie, and for being a good sport about how the movie turned out. It had a snakeskin strap like the jacket Cage had worn in an earlier, more prestigious movie, the jacket that symbolized his individuality, and his belief in personal freedom—rules to live by. The face had a picture of the Bigelow Skunk Ape that gave me the willies whenever I checked the time. The beast's long arms formed the watch's hour and minute hands. Not to seem ungrateful, because the watch was pretty sweet, made sweeter by the fact that it'd come from Nicolas Cage . . . but after everything I'd been through, sometimes I felt I deserved more than just a watch, ticking to remind me time was slipping away.

Luckily I hadn't worn the watch to work that morning. It was waterproof, but I doubted that extended to piss-and-shit-proof. I checked the time and saw it was business hours; Harry Muffet's car dealership would still be open. Was I still mad enough with Muffet to pay him a visit . . . ?

You're goddamn right I was.

6.

Harry's Pre-Owned American Auto was located in the hazy gray area between the bad and worse sides of town. One look at Harry's fleet of cars and you could see why more people were buying foreign these days. The place was little more than an automobile graveyard. The chain link security fence was probably to prevent folks from junking their own clunkers here; if that happened, I figured Harry would've just slapped a sales sticker on the piece of shit.

Draped above the lot like patriotic cobwebs were ropes of red, white and blue plastic pennants, snapping tackily in the breeze. The mess of ropes was connected to an ancient Airstream trailer that looked like a big rusty toaster. Moored to the roof of the trailer was a twenty-foot tall balloon man. The balloon man's likeness to Harry was unmistakable. He wore a checkered sports coat and slacks, even sported Harry's trademark mustache and shit-eating grin. The giant balloon man was filled with helium, I knew this because every month or so he'd 'mysteriously' break free of his bonds and float above town like the Goodyear blimp. For Harry it was great free advertising.

I trucked down the wide central lane, bracketed

by banks of used-cars, and stopped outside the Airstream. The inflatable Harry loomed above me, grinning and swaying in the breeze, the mooring ropes creaking as he strained against his bonds like a chained King Kong. A bird had shit on the balloon giant's head and smeared Harry's grinning face with guano. Maybe another unsatisfied customer.

The sign on the trailer door said OFFICE. The trailer was pitching and rocking like the coin-operated spaceship outside the laundromat in town, where the mommas parked their rugrats while they did laundry. Squeals and smutty laughter echoed from the trailer as it rock n' rolled.

Blueballs were the least I owed Muffet; I hammered on the door.

The trailer abruptly stopped rocking and swayed to a standstill. I heard whispered voices and a frantic scramble for clothes. Then the trailer door swung open and Harry appeared. He was beet-red, panting for breath, tucking his shirttails into his slacks. Artfully zipping his fly with his wedding ring hand, he raked his other hand through the sweaty corkscrews of his hair, and then gave his fringe a Bobby Kennedy-flick. In the office behind him I saw a pretty young woman I guessed was Harry's secretary. She was hastily rearranging her desk clutter and straightening her blouse, which she was wearing inside out with the label poking up like cowlicked hair. Apparently I'd knocked while Harry was in mid-sentence: "—and be sure to bring me those papers to sign the moment they arrive, Miss Clemens."

It might've been a more convincing performance if

not for the bitch-in-heat stink baking from the trailer, Miss Clemens's brassiere draped over her desk lamp, and Muffet angling his hips to hide his hard-on.

He saw who I was and panic flashed across his face. Then he plastered a grin across his mug. "Reggie! You made it!" Like I was a long lost war buddy.

"No thanks to you," I said, and tossed his wallet at him.

It bounced off his shirt and left a stain. Seems like I hadn't cleaned all the muck off it, after all. I almost smiled. "You left this behind when you ran out on me."

Harry was crestfallen. "Ran out on you?" he said in disbelief. "Is—is that how it looked?"

"That's how it was."

He chuckled at how I'd got this all ass backwards. "Reggie . . ." he said. "As God is my witness, nothing could be further from the truth." He took a moment to invent the truth. "I had to race back to the office, was all. Poor Miss Clemens here was holding the fort by her lonesome. I only stepped out for a quick bite to eat—" A beer and a lap dance must have been Muffet's idea of a power lunch. "When that ruffian attacked me. Without provocation, I might add."

"Then it's not true what Otis said about his sister?"

He dismissed my pedantry with a wave of his hand. "Let's not dwell on that."

He leaned towards me and whispered, "Is he dead?"

"You mean Otis? Of course he's not dead."

Harry looked disappointed.

"You think I'd just up and kill a man? I'm a bouncer, not a stone-cold killer."

"The way I hear it, you have before . . . Killed, I mean."

"That was different. That was self-defense."

"Even the orangutan?"

"*Especially* the orangutan."

Just then a plump gray rat darted from the trailer, claws clicking on the asphalt as it scuttled towards me. It clamped itself to my ankle and started humping my foot furiously, like the world was about to end and it wanted to go out fucking. With a cry of disgust, I started shaking my leg like Chuck Berry doing the duck-walk, but couldn't dislodge the critter.

Then I realized it wasn't a rat; no, that would be an insult to rats.

It was a dog—the ugliest fucking dog I'd ever seen in my life—a Chinese crested terrier. I'm more of an American bulldog man myself. Or a cat, if my only other canine option is a Chinese crested terrier.

The beast's hairless body was a sickly plucked-pink, spackled with markings like liver spots. The straggly gray fur of its mane, tail and booties had been groomed like a My Little Pony from hell. It pumped away at my foot, emitting high-pitched yipping noises with each thrust. Its eyes were narrowed to lusty slits. A stub of pink tongue poked between snaggly yellow fangs.

I could feel a damp patch developing on my ankle.

Harry chuckled, a little too indulgently for my liking. "Quit that, Gizmo."

He clawed the little beast from my foot and tucked

it under his arm. The dog started angrily yipping at me, as if I was a tease playing hard to get.

"Cute dog," I lied, frowning at the semen stain on my shoe. "Gizmo?"

"Like the movie," Harry said. "You know, don't feed 'em after midnight?"

"Looks like someone already has."

He glanced at the ugly little monster squirming under his arm. "What can I say? It's my wife's dog. Sometimes I think she loves this damn mutt more than me."

"Hard to believe." Actually, it was pretty easy. The dog's yipping was giving me a headache. "Listen, Muffet—"

"Hey! Call me Harry—"

"Muffet," I said. "I just came to return your wallet."

"A regular boy scout."

"Not really. You'll find it's light. I reimbursed myself the cost of a new shirt and pants." The soiled shorts were gratis, but he didn't need to know that. "Plus a copy of *Ring* magazine." I grinned. "That okay with you, Muffet?"

He peeked inside his empty wallet and winced. "Hell, it was the least I could do." He almost sounded magnanimous, as if he'd coughed up the dough himself.

I said, "And you can bet your ass Walt will be in touch with the bill for the damages."

He paled. "Damages?"

"About a men's room worth," I said, and then I doffed the brim of an imaginary hat. "Fuck you very much, Mr. Muffet. You have yourself a shitty day."

I started back to my truck.

"Reggie, wait—"

I stopped, sighed, slowly turned around.

"I feel terrible about what happened," he said. "Just plain terrible."

"Yeah, well. I'm sure Miss Clemens will lend you a shoulder to cry on."

He chuckled sheepishly and quickly changed tack. "You know, I followed your boxing career."

"Is that a fact?"

"Oh, sure. The Bear Hug Brannigan fight—"

"Boar Hog Brannon—"

"Helluva fight," he said, without skipping a beat.

I figured the extent of his knowledge about my boxing career came from the news cutting on the wall of The Henhouse. "You know I lost that one, right?"

"Well, sure. It was a close fight."

"Not really. Unless you count when he broke his hand on my head."

"All the same, I could use a man like you."

"For what? Protecting you from disgruntled customers?"

"No, no. Nothing like that. What happened with Otis was an aberration."

I strongly doubted that.

But against my better judgment, I said, "What exactly did you have in mind?"

TWO

JOHN WAYNE WAS A FAG

1.

Harry and me were huddled in my Ford, in a bad neighborhood, hidden in the shadows between two moth-haloed streetlamps. We were parked across the street from the debtor's clapboard bungalow, on a narrow street of identical dirt-poor domiciles. The red Caddy Eldorado was perched at the peak of the debtor's sharply sloping drive. Jewels of moonlight glinted off the windows. Harry was ogling the Caddy like a lion who's spotted a lame antelope wander from the herd. Me, I was frowning at the debtor's paperwork pinned to my clipboard, which the old woman—Dorothea Antwone, 67—had filled out when Harry sold her the Caddy on layaway.

It was my first week on the job and I still had newbie nerves.

Walt wasn't happy when he learned I was moon-lighting as Harry's repo man.

"You've already got a job," he'd complained. I said, "And maybe if you paid me a living wage, I wouldn't need another one." He said, "*Another* raise? In *this* economy?" I said, "The hell d'you mean 'another' raise?" The threat of raising my wage quickly put an end to the matter; Walt had grudgingly given me his blessing.

I put away Mrs. Antwone's paperwork. "I don't know about this one, Harry."

He tore his eyes away from the Eldorado. "What's the problem *this* time?"

"She's—what—only two weeks behind on her payments?"

"I should let things get out of hand?"

"You said she's a nurse."

"I said she works in a hospital."

"Probably she needs the car to get to work."

"Yeah?"

"It could mean someone's life."

"Oh, please! She's a cafeteria worker, for chris-sakes, not Florence Nightingale."

"What the hell are you doing selling a Cadillac Eldorado to a cafeteria worker?"

"It took some convincing, lemme tell you."

"But you must have known she wouldn't make her payments."

He grinned. "I suspected."

I shook my head at him. "You're some piece of work, Harry."

"Thanks."

"That wasn't a compliment."

But I had to hand it him. Harry must have been *some* kind of salesman. How else could he have sold me on taking this rotten job? Or maybe I was finally learning to take every opportunity that came my way, no matter how dubious.

"Your concern's duly noted," Harry told me. "Now c'mon, c'mon, c'mon."

With a heavy sigh, I climbed from the truck and glanced up and down the quiet street. In the movies, they called this kind of quiet, *too* quiet. Seeing nothing out of the ordinary—apart from me—I crossed the street, ducking into a crouch as I approached Mrs. Antwone's bungalow. Perched on the neighbor's porch rail was a raccoon, his burglar-masked eyes mocking my clumsy attempt at stealth.

I crept up the steeply sloping drive on the balls of my feet. Unsheathing the slimjim from inside my coat, I wedged the tool down inside the window frame and popped the door lock. A slimjim wouldn't work on a modern car. But for Harry's ancient fleet—'vintage,' he called them, once I even heard him use the word 'classic'—the tool worked like a charm.

I opened the door with a leather-gloved hand. The rusty hinges squealed like Freddy Kruegar raking his claws across sheet metal. Even the raccoon winced at the noise. I shot a peeved glance back at Harry—would it have killed him to oil the doors? Harry grinned and gave me a thumbs-up. I climbed inside the car. It still had that stale, secondhand showroom smell.

Harry had dismissed Mrs. Antwone as "just some

old broad, nothing for you to worry about." She'd taped a photo of her grandkids to the inside of the sun visor. A Christ-on-His-cross religious ornament dangled from the rearview mirror. Seeing Christ's agonized features gave me a moment's pause. I'm a God-fearing man, and I have every right to fear Him; the sonofabitch enjoys tormenting me like a cat with a broke-backed mouse. Silently begging His forgiveness for what I was about to do, I slid my skeleton key into the ignition, and was turning the engine—

When a voice from the backseat said: "Bitch, I got you now."

2.

Startling in surprise, I damn near filled my shorts again—and I hadn't even eaten microwave burrito. There was no time to turn around. I glanced in the rearview and saw a ninja behind me. Before I could make sense of what I was seeing, the ninja lunged forwards, looped a length of cord over the headrest and around my neck and then hauled back on it.

Reflexively raising my hand, I managed to slip my fingers inside the noose before it snared tight around my throat. The cord crushed my hand against my larynx, mashing my fingers, my pinkie snapping like a stick of chalk. Choking, I tried to cry out—in pain, and to Harry for help—but could only produce a series of pitiful spluttering sounds, like Donald Duck cussing his nephews.

The back of my head was pinned fast to the

headrest, tethering me to the seat. Unable to turn my head, I fidgeted wildly, watching helplessly in the rearview as the black-clad assassin garroted the life from me. I could see his eyes through the slit in his mask. He seemed surprised to see me. Maybe not as surprised as *I* was to see *him*, but close. It was as if he'd expected to be strangling someone else. I would've gladly switched places with his intended victim—I'm agreeable that way—and attempted to communicate this to the ninja in my Donald Duck voice. With my free hand, I slapped the steering wheel like a mixed martial artist tapping out of a cage fight. The car horn warbled an off-key verse of *La Cucaracha*. All of Harry's cars came with a melodic horn. He saw it as a classy selling point—

And where the fuck was Harry anyway?

As if in answer to my prayers, I heard the familiar phlegmatic roar of my truck engine. I glanced in the wing mirror. Across the street, I saw Harry behind the wheel of my Ford, gunning the engine like a drag racer at the starting line. I would have sighed with relief if only the ninja had let me breathe.

Thank God . . .

The cavalry was coming—

No . . .

The cavalry was driving away in my fucking truck!

I watched in disbelief as Harry burned rubber down the street. I pictured him hightailing it back to the lot, maybe saying a quick prayer for me before he slapped a sales sticker on my truck.

My fury at Harry gave me newfound strength. I

should have let Otis drown him in the crapper when I had the chance; hell, he should have been drowned in a crapper at birth. I was determined to survive, if only to kill the bastard.

With my free hand, I reached down the side of my seat, gripped the seat adjustor and cranked the handle, and then pushed my legs hard against the footwell. The seat shot backwards and crunched into the ninja's shins. He howled in pain. The pressure of the cord around my throat relaxed momentarily. I sucked a desperate gulp of air. But my triumph was short-lived. It usually is.

The bungalow's porch light blinked on. The front door clattered open and an elderly black woman charged from the house like a rheumatic rhino. She was wearing a floral nightdress, sleeping cap and slippers, and wielding a Dirty Harry hand cannon that was almost as big as her, cussing and calling me names she'd repent for in church, just as soon as she'd blown my head clean off. I guessed she couldn't see the ninja behind me, dressed all in black as he was.

Mrs. Antwone fired a wild shot from the .44 that punched through the windshield and thudded into the passenger seat. A blizzard of seat stuffing stormed through the car. The recoil knocked the old girl out of her slippers. She clambered back to her feet and fired another shot that sheared away the driver's-side wing mirror in a flash of sparks.

The ninja ducked down behind me and cried, "Shit!"

One of us had to, I was still being strangled.

This time, Mrs. Antwone planted her feet and

took careful aim.

I was dead in her sights.

Her finger teased the trigger—

Using my free hand, I yanked the handbrake. The brakes unlocked with a squeal. The Eldorado gave a violent jerk and swooped away down the drive like a ship being launched. Mrs. Antwone's shot ricocheted off the roof. The Caddy continued rolling in reverse down the drive, crashing through trashcans like it was bowling a strike, reaching warp speed as it rocketed across the street, and plowed into a Buick that was parked on the opposite curb. We jolted to a sudden stop that whiplashed my neck and hurled the ninja forwards from the backseat.

He butted the back of my headrest with nose-crunching force. The cord went slack around my throat. I clawed it away and heaved for breath. Then I turned towards him, balling the front of his shirt in one fist while I clobbered him unconscious with the other. I let him go and he slumped back on the seat.

In the orange glow of the streetlamps, and the houselights blinking on along the street, I could see that the ninja was in fact just a wiry little guy wearing a biker's balaclava and all-black clothes. As I was about to remove his mask—

Headlights blinded me, and I glanced up and saw a speeding truck bearing down on me . . .

My truck.

There was Harry at the wheel, a look of grim determination on his face. Even over the rising roar of the engine, I could hear him yelling, "Hold on, Reggie! I'm coming!"

"Harry, no, wait—!"

The truck broadsided the Caddy and flipped it like a pancake. The ninja and me were tossed about the car like socks on a spin cycle. The Caddy came crashing down on its roof, skidding along the street, spitting sparks in its wake. When we finally scraped to a seesawing stop, I could hear the ninja groaning somewhere in the upturned car behind me. I bellied through the broken driver's-side window. Diamonds of Plexiglas studded my forearms as I slithered from the wreckage and collapsed on someone's lawn. A plastic yard flamingo loomed above me like a fabulous pink carrion bird. I caught my breath, and then forced myself to sit, and then a shrill voice cried, "Dirty no-good car-stealin' motherfucker!" And then the harmless old broad whacked me upside the head with the butt of her Magnum, and it was lights out.

* * *

When I regained consciousness, stretched across the lawn, Harry was kneeling beside me, squeezing my hand. The hand with the broken fingers. It hurt; it hurt a great deal. I tried to tell him this, but could only whimper. "Reggie?" he was saying. "You okay, Reggie? Squeeze my hand if you can hear me, buddy." He gave my mitt another hard squeeze and I made a noise like bathwater gurgling down the plughole.

I heard the old woman's voice. "Mr. Muffet?" She sounded surprised to see him, and embarrassed he was seeing her in her nightclothes. "Oh, my goodness. That reminds me. I plain forgot to make my car payments this month."

"I'd be happy to hold your firearm while you write me a check, Mrs. Antwone."

"Huh-Harry . . ." I croaked.

He gave my injured hand another long, hard squeeze.

"Right here, big guy. Save your strength. You can thank me later."

"I quit."

3.

The ninja's name was Charles Eustace Cluley. He had murdered four women in the tri-state area over the past two years. His M.O. was always the same. After breaking into the victim's car, Cluley would hide in the backseat, waiting patiently for the female owner to return—and then throttle them to death with a length of cord. Dorothea Antwone was fixing to be his fifth victim when I bumbled along and fritzed the deal. Her murder would have brought him over the top, made him a bona fide serial killer. And with that hope in mind, the press had already given him a name: The Backseat Strangler. Not the most remarkable moniker. But then, Charles Eustace Cluley, when he wasn't killing women, was by and large an unremarkable man. The kind of fella neighbors described as a quiet man, who kept to himself, *if* they even noticed him at all . . .

Constable Randy-Ray Gooch said: "And none of this rings any bells with you?"

I just blinked at Gooch lazily, smiling a sloppy smile. I was doped with so many meds, I felt like I was floating above the hospital bed like the possessed girl in *The Exorcist*. My hand wore a cotton glove of bandages; my arm looked like a giant Q-tip. A painful knot pulsated on the back of my skull where Mrs. Antwone had brained me with her Magnum. My neck was cocooned in a brace.

I vaguely recalled seeing the Backseat Strangler mentioned in the *Bugle* as I'd flipped to the sports section and the funnies. And of course, I remembered Sherlock Wiley confidently predicting the offender would be Mexican; Walt was as good a psychological profiler as he was a stockbroker, because Charles Eustace Cluley was about as Mexican as I am.

I reassured Gooch I'd been listening.

"Buzz . . . seed . . . strong . . . laaaa . . ." I slurred, when attempts to communicate by telepathy failed. Then I started giggling like a Japanese schoolgirl.

Gooch shook his head. "What the hell kinda meds they got you on?"

I was still grinning at Gooch when we heard what sounded like an angry bear stomping down the hospital corridor towards my room.

"Levine!" the bear was roaring. "Reggie Levine!"

I stopped grinning. The angry bear was killing my high.

Gooch sighed. "In here, chief."

Craw County Sheriff, Newman Jaynes, was a heavyset man with a steel-gray flattop, steelier grayer eyes, and a craggy Mount Rushmore mug. His hand rarely left the butt of his holstered sidearm; like one of the barflies leaning with his elbow on the slab at The Henhouse. We seldom saw Jaynes in Bigelow—except around election time—Gooch boasted this was due to his efficiency as town constable. In my dealings with Jaynes, in the aftermath of the skunk ape thing, I got the impression that he considered Bigelow and her people as his cross to bear, like he was the sheriff of the Twilight Zone. I guess I could see his point.

Jaynes stormed into the room. The angry look on his face, I wondered had he got the wrong room and somehow mistaken me for the Strangler? "Levine, you stupid sonofabitch!"

Nope, he had the right room. Well, shit. I hadn't been expecting no medal, but a simple thank you for apprehending a vicious serial killer would've been nice.

Gooch said, "Take it easy now, chief—"

Jaynes glanced at Gooch and cried out in disgust and hurriedly averted his eyes.

"What the hell, Randy-Ray!"

Now I should probably mention that Gooch was not at the hospital solely in an official capacity. He was a patient himself, having suffered an allergic reaction to a batch of counterfeit laundry detergent. Martha Gooch had bought the bootleg Tide from a bucket seller, and washed her husband's jockey shorts in it. Gooch's testicles had molted and then swollen to the size of grapefruits, necessitating the use of a truss I can only describe as a gauze mankini; he was wearing what looked like a cross between The

Mummy and Sean Connery's bandolier-diaper in *Zardoz*. Until Jaynes's disgusted reaction, I hadn't been sure I wasn't hallucinating the whole thing.

"Damn it, man!" Jaynes said to Gooch. "Would you cover yourself?"

Gooch closed his hospital gown, tying the sash loosely around his waist.

"The doc told me I need to air myself regular," he muttered sheepishly.

Looming over my bed, Jaynes glared down at me like I was something he'd scraped off the bottom of his shoe. "You gonna live?"

I mustered my most shit-eating grin. "You should see the other guy."

Jaynes bristled with anger. "I *have* seen the other guy. What's left of him. Thanks to the excessive force you and Muffet used when you made your little citizen's arrest—and that's putting it fucking mildly—the Strangler's lawyer reckons he's got a good shot at getting the charges dropped against his client. That kill-crazy maniac could be walking the streets again, instead of riding the lightning like he so richly deserves. I've half a mind to lock you and Muffet in a room with the victims' families, let 'em beat the living dogshit outta you clowns!"

Jaynes stabbed a finger in my face. "You just better hope and pray that Strangler sonofabitch doesn't sue the county. And I don't ever wanna hear your name in my office again, Levine. I mean, *ever!* I hear you've so much as farted in church, I'll come down on you like you won't believe. You'll be sharing a cell with Steven Avery. Are we clear?"

He turned his finger towards Gooch.

"Keep this dumb bastard away from me, Gooch."

And with that, Jaynes stormed from the room. When his footsteps faded away down the corridor, Gooch sighed. "For what it's worth," he said, "I reckon you done good, son." He gave my shoulder a comradely squeeze, and then he waddled from the room like a pregnant duck, and left me to take a nap.

4.

Mrs. Antwone woke me around noon with one of her "special lunches." The old dear had returned to work at the hospital cafeteria directly after giving her statement to the law. "I never missed a day of work in my life, and I ain't about to start now, Strangler be damned." She told me she felt terrible about pistol-whipping me—which was probably not as terrible as I felt, being on the receiving end—and was eager to make it up to me. How she hoped to achieve that by poisoning me with her cooking, like a culinary Angel of Death, I didn't know.

She placed the tray of food on the nightstand. I said, "Really Mrs. Antwone, you shouldn't have." And I meant it. She'd already treated me to what she called her "hero's breakfast." I'd thought that microwave burrito was bad, but at least I'd required a solid punch in the guts before I soiled myself.

"You got a visitor, Mr. Levine," she said.

I sighed, hoping Sheriff Jaynes hadn't returned to bawl me out again.

Then a familiar voice said: "How's it hanging, champ?"

Harry stood in the doorway with a big bouquet of flowers.

Mrs. Antwone smiled at us both.

"My heroes . . . I'll leave you boys some privacy."

I almost begged her to stay.

Harry entered the room, clutching the bouquet before him like a shield.

"What are you doing here, Muffet?"

"Well, I pride myself on being a caring employer."

He placed the flowers on my bed, like he was laying a wreath upon a grave.

"I told you, right after you damn near killed me: I quit."

"You were serious about that? I figured you were in shock."

"I was," I said. "But I still meant it. Now get the hell out of here before I call security." I was in no fit state to kick his ass, much as I dearly wanted to. I picked up the flowers and thrust them at him. "And take your damn flowers with you." I glanced at the card on the bouquet. "And who the hell is Mrs. Yakamoto?"

"Room 237," Harry said. "I figured you'd get more use out of them." He crossed himself.

The last thing I needed was a clan of angry Yakuza hunting for whoever stole their mama-san's flowers. I shook my head at him. "You really are some piece of—"

"Work?"

"No."

"Alright, I can tell you're a little sore."

"I'm a lot sore, not to mention I hurt like holy fucking hell."

"So I'll come back when you're a little less cranky."

I hurled a bedpan at his head and he ducked and it clanged off the wall as he scuttled out the door.

But if I thought that was the last I'd ever see of Harry Muffet, that from herein my life would be jake, then I was sorely, believe me, *sorely* mistaken.

THREE

GOATSUCKER

1.

A week or two later and mostly healed, I was back at work at The Henhouse.

"Where you belong," Walt had said, in a welcome-back speech that chilled me to the core. Christ, there had to be more than *this* . . . Didn't there?

I was playing the *Smokey and the Bandit* pinball machine, on my last ball. Despite my poorly paw—my pinkie and ring fingers were splinted and taped together, my hand wore a glove of bruises—I was really racking up the points and feeling confident I could reclaim my high score from my rival pinball wizard.

That's when the phone in the phone kiosk started ringing.

"Phone," Walt said to me. He might've snapped his fingers too, but he was otherwise engaged, experimenting with the recipe for a twenty-dollar cocktail he called the Skunk Ape; so far all he'd got right was the smell.

"Can't you get it?" I whined, struggling to concentrate on my game.

"Why don't you ask your friend Harry to get it?" Walt said.

I'd heard a lot of that shit since I came back to work. Why don't you ask your friend Harry to do *this*, why don't you ask your friend Harry to do *that*; why don't you ask your friend Harry to pay your paycheck this week? I guess I should've been flattered Walt was jealous.

The phone continued ringing. Finally old Lou gave a burdened sigh, dragged himself from his spot at the end of the stage, and crossed the room to answer the phone. Lou wasn't being helpful so much as the noise was distracting him from Marlene's performance. "Henhouse, Louis speaking." Lou listened to the caller and then suddenly gasped. He muffled the mouthpiece. "Reggie, it's for you." Lou's eyes were shining with the kind of excitement he usually reserved for when Marlene shucked her drawers.

"Take a message."

"But—but Reggie . . . it's Nicolas Cage."

I said, "Huh?" Taking my eyes off the playfield and losing my last pinball.

"Damn it!" I said, and smacked the machine. The automated voice of Jackie Gleason mocked me from the machine: "Nobody, and I mean *nobody* makes Sheriff Buford T. Justice look like a possum's pecker!"

Walt looked a little disappointed he hadn't answered the phone himself. He could've chewed the fat with his buddy 'Nick.' "Maybe he wants to make another movie about this Backseat Strangler thing?"

Great. First the skunk ape thing, now the Backseat Strangler thing.

I went and took the phone from Lou, shooing him away when he tried to eavesdrop. I brushed down my shirt, ran a hand through my hair—I don't know why, it wasn't like Cage could see me—cleared my throat and said, "Mr. Cage, it's an honor to finally—"

Harry cut in and said, "I apologize for the subterfuge, Reggie. But you wouldn't return my calls, and I took Mr. Wiley at his word that he'd shoot me if I showed my face at The Henhouse."

"Harry?" I cut a sorry glance at the pinball machine. "You sonofabitch!"

"Don't hang up, Reggie. Please!"

To this day, I don't know why I didn't hang up the phone then and there. Maybe it was the desperation in his voice, and the part of me that liked hearing it.

"I need your help," he said.

"You need help alright."

"I'm in trouble here, Reggie. Big trouble."

"And I should give a shit *why* exactly?"

"I thought we were friends?"

I hacked a bitter laugh. "What the hell gave you that idea?"

He quickly changed tack; he had a way of doing that, a way I can only describe as Muffetish. "Well, you ungrateful bastard. Now I'm not the kinda guy who calls in favors . . . But—well—you owe me."

"How do you figure that?"

"It wasn't for me, that Strangler sonofabitch

might've strangled you."

"I'd already kayoed him when you rammed me with my truck! Besides, it wasn't for you, I wouldn't have been there to be strangled to start with."

"Oh, now you're just splitting hairs."

"Not to mention I'd still have my truck."

"Is that what this is about?"

"This, what? *You* called *me!*"

"You want a truck? Come to the lot, you can pick out any damn truck you like!"

He'd baited the hook; I couldn't resist. "Any truck?"

"Any truck. In fact, I've got just the truck for you."

"You just said I could pick."

"Yeah, but, Reggie—once you *see* this truck, you won't *want* any other one."

I gave a long sigh. "Exactly what kinda trouble are you in, Muffet?"

"The deep shit kind."

I gave a knowing grunt.

"Come to the lot, I'll tell you everything."

"And you'll give me a truck—" I reminded him, but he'd already hung up.

I put the phone down, and returned to the pinball machine.

"Well?" Walt said. "What'd he say?"

"Your buddy, 'Nick'? He wants you to be in his next movie."

Walt nearly dropped the liquor bottle he was holding. "Holy—He said that?"

"'Course, he says you'll have to lose some weight."

Walt sucked in his gut. "I'm working on that already," he bullshitted. "The last few pounds, I can always borrow some of Marlene's diet pills."

Oh, yeah. Those pills were working wonders for Marlene.

"And you'll have to wear a hairpiece," I said.

Walt squeaked a hand across his shiny bald dome. His eyes narrowed in suspicion. "Wasn't him, was it?"

I laughed, and he pitched a bar towel at me. "Not cool, Levine!"

"It was Muffet," I told him. "Says he's in some kinda trouble, thinks I can help."

"What kinda trouble?"

"The deep shit kind was all he'd say on the phone."

"Heh. Your specialty."

"Not by choice."

"Maybe you oughta go see him."

"How's that?"

"The cocksucker's check for the damage to the men's room bounced."

"I warned you, that's your own damn fault for taking a check from him."

"I'd sure hate for something to happen to him before he pays what he owes."

"You're all heart, Walt."

"I hear that a lot."

2.

Later that afternoon, I bummed a ride from Lou, who was heading home to freshen up before he returned to The Henhouse for the late show. Lou dropped me off outside Harry's Pre-Owned American Auto, tooting his horn as he tootled away in his mustard-colored Gremlin. Walking through the dealership lot, the first thing I noticed, there wasn't a truck in sight—it was like there'd been a truck pogrom—except for the old beater Jeep Wagoneer parked prominently outside Harry's trailer office. *Any truck on the lot, my punchy ass.*

Harry scuttled from the trailer. "Reggie! I knew you'd come!"

"That makes one of us."

"So," he said, gesturing grandly at my 'new' truck, "whaddya think?"

"That I wasted my time coming here." I inspected the Jeep. "Is that rust?"

"Hell, no. That's character. And just wait till you hear her. She roars like the MGM lion." I thought it more likely she death-rattled like the lion that prick dentist shot. "Now before you take her for a spin, come inside."

He clutched my arm and dragged me inside the trailer.

My feet braced themselves to be bushwhacked by Harry's ugly fucking dog. I couldn't see the mutt anywhere, but that didn't mean the little monster wasn't lurking, biding his time and waiting for me to lower my guard.

"No Miss Clemens?" I said.

She must've clocked out; her brassiere wasn't hanging from her desk lamp.

"I gave her some time off till I get this business straightened out."

Harry sank down with a sigh into the faux leather recliner behind his desk. The American flag was draped across the wall behind him. On the desk, a cheap plastic bust of a bald eagle was pinning down a stack of PAST DUE bills. There was also a framed photo of Harry and his wife standing proudly outside the dealership. Mrs. Muffet was a heavyset woman with a beehive hairdo and a face like the swarm had attacked it. She was wearing a gaudy rhinestone pantsuit that even Liberace would've thought excessive. The ugly fucking dog was clutched against her huge bosom like a canine mountaineer buried in a glittery avalanche.

On the wall was a rack of car keys; a crumpled single dollar in a glass display case, presumably the first buck Muffet ever swindled off a sucker; and a shrine of photos showing Harry shaking hands with a bunch of satisfied customers. A number of photos had been removed from the shrine, like a jigsaw puzzle with missing pieces. I figured these must have been customers whose satisfaction soured shortly after driving their new secondhand wheels off the lot.

In the corner of the trailer was a plush velvet pillow. Regal-red, coated in dog hair, indented with the little mutt's impression. There was still no sign of Gizmo anywhere and my feet began to relax. Next to the pillow were bowls for food and water. On the shelf above it were doggie treats that probably cost more than my monthly grocery bill, gnarly chew toys, and an array of dog grooming products. There was also a trophy that looked like a gilded *Monopoly* dog. I took a closer look at the trophy inscription. "That—*thing* won a dog show?"

"Won a bunch of 'em in his day," Harry said. "'Course he's past prime now."

"I know the feeling."

"But he still rakes in the bucks as a stud."

And there the similarities between Gizmo and me ended.

Harry swiveled his recliner towards a filing cabinet and pulled a half-empty whiskey bottle from the bottom drawer. He raised his eyebrow at me. I knew it was an old salesman's trick. Get the mark loaded before talking turkey. All the same, I nodded. He poured us drinks, gave me my Dixie cup, and gestured for me to sit.

"So what's the big emergency?" I said.

I could see him thinking how best to phrase it.

In the end, he must've figured: *Fuck it.*

He came right out with, "Are you familiar with the chupacabra?"

I was; after the skunk ape thing, I'd made it my business to bone up on my cryptozoology. Some people say the chupacabra is a wild, devil-dog; others, that it's some kind of reptile; most right-minded folks say the legend is a crock of shit. Whatever the damned thing is, it's believed to be responsible for a spate of cattle mutilations across the Southern states, in which the victims, often goats, are drained of blood. This has given the chupacabra its name, which in American translates to 'goatsucker.'

I was starting to feel like a sucker myself.

I downed my drink, stood up to leave. "I knew this was a waste of time—"

"Wait!" He rooted through his desk drawers and fished out an advertising flyer.

I looked at the flyer. At Gizmo's empty pillow. Back at Harry. "What the fuck?"

Harry choked down the lump in his throat and nodded.

The flyer read:

GRABOWSKI'S GAS & ZOO
AS READ ABOUT IN THE WEEKLY WORLD NEWS
REAL! LIVE! CHUPACABRA!

Below the text was a grainy black and white Xerox of Gizmo that didn't do justice to the ugly fucking dog's fucking ugliness.

"Well, I can see why a person would be confused." Harry frowned at me. "It's an ugly fucking dog, Harry." He opened his mouth to object before ceding the point with a nod. "How exactly did this happen?" I asked him.

"Wipe that smirk off your face, I'll tell you."

He poured us another drink.

"Miss Clemens and I were working late—"

"Burning the old midnight oil, huh?"

"You wanna hear this or not?"

I mimed zipping my lips.

"As you may have noticed," Harry said, "the AC's on the fritz."

I *had* noticed. The trailer was stifling hot, not to mention choked with the stench of dog and all those late nights Harry worked with Miss Clemens.

"So the other night, we're working late, and it's hot

as hell up in here. I opened the windows, wedged the door open to get some air inside. I swear I only took my eyes off him for a second. Well . . . Five minutes, at least."

I raised my Dixie cup in admiration.

Men our age, pushing forty, five minutes wasn't bad going.

"By the time I even realized he was missing, Gizmo was gone, doggy, gone."

"And you think this Grabowski guy stole him?"

"Hell, I don't know. I'll admit, there's a little bad blood between us."

"You sold him a car, didn't you?"

"I can't be held responsible once the car leaves the lot!"

"You ought to make that your slogan," I said. "Look. I don't see what you expect me to do here, Muffet. I mean, it's a funny story and all—"

"Funny? I'm happy as hell you're getting a kick out of it, Reggie. But if my wife finds out I lost Gizmo, not to mention he's currently the star attraction at a roadside zoo, I am a fucking dead man. She'll bury me sans balls in Potter's field. Reggie . . . Everything I got, every damn red cent, it's all in that evil witch's name." He gave his hair a Bobby Kennedy-flick. "For business reasons."

"And where is the little lady?"

Harry shuddered. "There's nothing little or ladylike about that woman. Right now she's in London, England. Chairing some kinda Kennel Club conference. The only reason she didn't take Gizmo with her, the limeys would've quarantined him. She couldn't bear it."

"When are you expecting her back?"

"End of the week."

"Plenty of time for you to bring in the law," I said. "Go see Randy-Ray." A story like this might take Gooch's mind off his swollen balls. If he didn't laugh 'em off.

Harry shook his head. "Can't risk it. The wife's friendly with Mrs. Gooch. And you know how Randy-Ray likes to flap his jaw. No way she wouldn't find out."

"Then I don't know what else to suggest."

He raised his hand like a kid in class. "Can I make a suggestion?"

"Not if it involves me getting involved."

He lowered his hand. "But—but you help people, don't you?"

Here we went with that one-man *A-Team* shit again.

"I don't know where the hell people got that idea."

"You helped Ned Pratt."

"I'd had the slightest idea what I was getting myself into, I wouldn't have."

"But this isn't like that skunk ape thing!"

"Oh, give it time."

"All I'm asking you here—and I really don't think it's too much to ask of a guy whose life I saved—all I'm asking is for you to get Gizmo back from Grabowski."

"You make it sound easy."

"It *is* easy!"

"That's what worries me," I said. "What's this Grabowski like?"

"Old," he said. "Nothing for you to worry about."

"Like Mrs. Antwone and her .44 Magnum."

"Alright. So he ain't exactly a people person. In fact he's a crotchety sonofabitch. But he's harmless enough. He won't try and plug you." He considered this. "I mean, not unless you give him good reason."

"Like if I try and take his chupacabra away?"

Harry gave a nervous laugh and slugged his drink.

I chewed it over some. Maybe it was Gizmo's name, but I remembered a line from an old movie: *With Mogwai comes much responsibility . . .* That went double with being a hero. I'm not saying that's how I saw myself. But after the skunk ape thing, others did. And I'll admit, it flattered me. Ever since the Boar Hog Brannon fight, after which I'd been forced to hang up my boxing gloves, I'd been the nearly man, the coulda-shoulda-woulda guy. The skunk ape thing changed all that. People started looking at me different. I felt a certain pressure to live up to the legend. I mostly didn't mind helping folks out. Teaching an abusive husband some manners, or a bullied kid some moves; it made me feel more useful than ejecting a drunk from The Henhouse. So getting Harry's ugly fucking dog back seemed to be cinch. What was the worst could happen?

I gave a long sigh. "If I do this—"

"God bless you, Reggie!"

"I've got some conditions."

His smile disappeared and his eyes became guarded. "I'm listening."

"I want you to pay Walt what you owe for the damage to the men's room."

"Is that all? No problem! I'll write him a check right now."

"Cash."

"I—I don't have that kinda money lying around."

"Sure you do. A guy like you always keeps a get-away stash."

"A guy like me? The hell's that supposed to mean?"

"Let's keep this civil, huh."

He gave a heavy sigh of resignation. "Anything else?"

"Yeah," I said. "You're coming with me."

"But—but that kinda defeats the purpose of me sending you."

"Non-negotiable, Muffet."

He threw up his hands in surrender. "Fine!"

"And we'll take my new truck," I told him. "It doesn't make the trip to Grabowski's and back, then the deal's off, you're on your own."

He wet his mustache with a nervous flick of his tongue.

"Maybe we oughta take my car?"

3.

We took old highway 9 out to Grabowski's Gas & Zoo.

Since the interstate opened, the old highway had been left to rack and ruin. It looked like a scene from a post-apocalyptic road movie. The blacktop was cracked and cratered and sprouting weeds, and the Sticks were closing in on either side, eager to reclaim the land for Mother Nature.

Harry seemed even more surprised than me that the Jeep had made it this far.

As if worried the truck would crap out at any moment, and I'd abandon him, he was nervously prattling away about what a sweet ride she was; that he had to be crazy to just give her away; but that's the kinda guy he was, generous to a fault—

I turned on the radio to drown out his voice. The dial came off in my hand. "Look at frigging Superman over here!" Harry chuckled. "Guy doesn't know his own strength." He snatched the dial from me and reattached it to the radio. "That's nothing a little superglue won't fix."

Up ahead was a sun-faded sign, hanging crookedly over the highway like a hitcher's thumb:

EAT—GAS—ZOO

"This is the place," Harry said.

"You think?"

There sure as hell wasn't anything else out here.

I pulled onto the cracked-dirt forecourt, kicking up a cloud of dust that swallowed the Jeep as I stopped alongside the rusted gas pumps. The dust ghosted away to reveal the filling station, a ramshackle clapboard cabin that sagged against the porch like a senior citizen clinging to his walking frame.

At the rear of the property was a corrugated sheet metal fence, painted with a mural of the animals being herded two by two into Noah's ark. The painting had all the artistic flair of a child's drawing stuck to a refrigerator door. The paint was peeling from the corrugated iron in the baking heat, the animals slowly fading into extinction.

There was no sign of human life anywhere.

I honked the horn for service, snatched the keys from the ignition and started climbing from the Jeep. Harry said, "You're taking the keys?" He'd disguised himself with sunglasses and a Bigelow Baboons cap, and was ducking down in his seat, hiding his face and just generally drawing attention to himself.

"Wouldn't want you getting itchy feet again," I told him.

I started towards the filling station.

A scrawny old man butted outside through the screen door, hiking his suspender straps over bony shoulders. A sweat-yellowed wifebeater clung to his cadaverous frame. His hair was a wispy white rat's-nest. His mouth was an angry pucker. With his sun-wrinkled face and scowl, he looked like a pissed-off California Raisin. But his blue eyes were clear and sharp as he sized me up.

"Mr. Grabowski?" I said.

"That you layin' on the damn horn?" he said, in a shrill old timer's voice. "Think I'm deaf or sumpin? Ain't nothin' wrong with my hearin'. It's my legs is the problem. Damn rheaumatiz. You'll find out, just you wait."

He cleared his throat loudly—sounded like a penny caught in a garbage disposal—before giving me his spiel: "Grill's broke, I don't got no gas, and the zoo tour's ten bucks." Then he held out his hand expectantly.

Quite the showman.

"I came to see the chupacabra," I told him, holding up the advertising flyer with Gizmo's picture on it.

The old man nodded like why the hell else would I be there?

"Chupacabra's part of the ten buck tour," he said.

"I couldn't just see the chupacabra for a buck?"

"No," he said firmly. "You could not."

I should've had Harry front me cash for expenses.

"C'mon, c'mon, c'mon . . ." the old man said, like he had other *paying* visitors lining up.

I rooted in my pockets for my wallet.

He took a closer study of me. "Hey," he said. "Ain't you that skunk ape idjit?"

Infamy has its perks. It had to be worth a free roadside zoo tour.

"Reggie Levine," I said, offering my hand. "Good to meetcha."

He crossed his arms. "Kilt an orangutan, as I recall."

"Sir," I said, "I hated to do it."

"And an itty bitty bear cub."

"The bear cub's just gossip. It was full grown and mean."

So much for my free tour. I dug out ten bucks. Knowing now he was dealing with Reggie Levine, the scourge of orangutans and itty bitty bear cubs, the old man considered the cash like it was blood money. "I oughta charge you twenty."

But despite his misgivings, he snatched the bill and pocketed it quicker than the gals at The Henhouse scalping a sucker. Then he turned towards the filling station and started shuffling inside with a soldier's follow-me gesture.

I glanced back at Harry, ducking below the Jeep's window line, and then followed the old man inside.

4.

The first thing that hit me was the animal stench: Phil Spector's Wall of Sound meets Smell-O-Vision. The air shimmered with stink-waves, like heat rising from the highway on a sweltering summer's day. Not wanting to be impolite, I tugged my shirt collar up over my nose and mouth and discreetly retched. Then there was the noise: A deafening live concert of *Old McDonald's Farm*. As if that Noah's ark mural had come to barking, bleating, bellowing life.

Critters of every description rampaged through the store's three aisles, looting the shelves like *Supermarket Sweep* contestants. A possum was perched on the store counter like he was manning the cash register. Squirrels scuttled across the wire clothes rack, where GRABOWSKI GAS & ZOO tee shirts were on sale. I ducked my head beneath a flock of parrots flying laps around the room. Rabbits fucked like rabbits every which way I looked. Cats brushed against my ankles and used my shins as scratching posts. A dog was pinching a loaf in the middle aisle, glaring at me over his shoulder as if to say: *You're so interested in watching me shit, how about you wipe my ass for me?* Behind the counter was an army surplus rack, where a fat pink sow was sleeping with the covers pulled up to her snout, snoring like a drunk at the end of a bender.

In short, if it walked or crawled, slithered or flew, it was walking and crawling and slithering and flying through the filling station store. About the only creature I *couldn't* see was a Chinese crested terrier cum chupacabra.

The floor was sheeted with old newspaper dating back to when the first Bush was President; the newspaper was covered with cat- and dog- and bird- and I don't know what else- shit, a large pile of which I had stepped in as I entered the store. "Don't tread that mess through here!" Grabowski barked at me. Like it would have made any kind of difference. I scraped the shit off the bottom of my shoe on another fossilized dog turd. Then I just gazed around the store in horror.

"Nice place," I said. "You, uh—get many visitors?"

"It's been a little slow lately," the old man admitted.

He nodded at the advertising flyer I was using to fan the air.

"But I'm hoping the chupacabra's gonna change that."

"How long you been open?"

"Since after the 'Nam."

Great, I thought. A Vietnam vet. That's all I needed.

"Thank you for your service, sir."

"A howler monkey saved my life in the war, you know," he added casually.

A *crazy* Vietnam vet. Thanks a fucking bunch, Harry.

"No kidding?"

"Son," he said. "One thing you'll learn about me right quick: I don't kid around."

He shuffled behind the store counter, shooing the possum away from the register. He opened the cash drawer and peered inside and then glanced at the possum as if he suspected it was skimming his profits. He put my ten bucks in the register and slammed the drawer shut.

"We was deep in-country," the old man said. "I was on point, leading my squad through the boonies, when this voice from the trees above me yells 'Grabby!' Grabby being short for Grabass. Which is what the fellas used to call me on account of what happened one night in a Saigon go-go bar. Used to, I oughta point out. You get the urge to call me Grabass . . . *don't*."

"The thought never even crossed my mind, sir."

He nodded. "So, I wheel around towards the voice, looking up in the trees where it come from, and I see this howler monkey looking down at me. I think, *Huh?* Cuz as far as I know, howler monkeys don't talk. Next thing I know a VC bullet comes whizzing past my head, close enough it nicks my earlobe. My head wasn't turned to look at the howler monkey, I woulda been a goner for sure. I yell to the squad, 'Ambush!' And everybody hits the deck and everything goes loud . . ."

The old man's eyes misted over. I could tell he was back in the jungle again.

Finally he said, "It wasn't for that howler monkey calling my name when he done, me and the whole squad woulda been fish-in-a-barrel for Charlie."

I nodded respectfully, hearing the *Twilight Zone* theme in my mind.

"What happened to the howler monkey?"

"Killed by friendly fire," he said, in a choked voice. He crossed himself and gazed to the heavens with watery eyes.

I couldn't help wondering if he'd been the friendly who pulled the trigger.

"Anyways," he said. "Thanks to that howler monkey, I made it back home in one piece. Figured I'd pay the favor forward, started taking in strays. At first it was mostly just cats and dogs. Not much chance of seein' no howler monkey here in Bigelow . . . Just skunk apes, right?" He winked at me slyly. "But before I knew it, folks was sending me critters I didn't even know the name for. First time I seen a kangaroo—part of the tour, by the way—I thought someone was funning me, searched him for the zipper and he socked me in the jaw and knocked out three teeth. Well, in the end I had to open the zoo to the paying public, just to keep 'em all watered and fed."

He reached beneath the counter and fetched up a rifle. Saw my expression and chuckled. "Relax, son. I wanted to kill you, you'd be dead already."

"That's a relief."

"Rifle's just a precaution."

"For what?"

"Tibby."

"Who's Tibby?"

"Tiberius," he said. "He's my Bengal."

I swallowed hard. "You—you've got a tiger back there?"

Grabowski grinned, missing three teeth courtesy of that kangaroo.

"This way for the tour, sir."

5.

When I saw Tiberius, I realized I needn't have worried. The mangy old Bengal was all skin and bones, lying slumped in his cage like a terminally ill Frosted Flakes mascot. One hearty cry of "*Grrrrreat!*" would finish the poor bastard off.

Grabowski loaded his rifle and aimed at the tiger. Thinking the old man meant for me to witness a mercy killing, I grabbed the barrel before he fired.

Grabowski frowned. "Want your pitcher took with him, don't you? You're welcome to put your arm around him without me doping him up first. Just don't expect to get your arm back."

I realized the rifle was a tranquilizer gun. "Is a photo included in the tour?" A picture of me with the tiger would sit nicely on the wall next to my *Rocky* poster.

"Hell, no. Five bucks."

"Then I'll pass," I said, reluctantly.

"Might've told me that before I loaded the tranq gun," he muttered.

He slung the rifle strap over his shoulder and we continued the tour.

Such as it was.

The zoo yard was a teeming favela of hutches and pens, and cages cemented to cinderblock slabs.

Shabby-looking petting animals, and disheveled barnyard beasts, wandered freely about a yard that was little bigger than a baseball diamond. For most of these wretched creatures, it had been a choice between Grabowski's Gas & Zoo or Stephen King's *Pet Sematary*.

I looked around for Gizmo, but still couldn't see the chupacabra enclosure.

What I did see was a jackass, hitched to a post inside a pen alongside the filling station store. He had a bluish-gray body, a white ruff of belly, and a gnarly black mane that was part Flock of Seagulls, part mullet. His tall, wonky ears reminded me of the antennae on an old TV with bad reception. He also had five legs.

Then I did another count of his limbs and said, "Holy shit!"

Grabowski followed my gaze and nodded, "It's something, ain't it?"

I said, "Holy shit!" again.

The jackass had what looked like a thick black anaconda snaking out from his undercarriage.

"Enrique's new here," Grabowski said. "Before he arrived, I never fully appreciated the term 'donkey-dicked.' I was tempted to advertise him on the flyer along with the chupacabra, but I couldn't figure out how to phrase it right."

I shook my head in awe. "Where'd you find him?"

"Doc Dubrow had him brung here from Mexico," Grabowski said.

As I've mentioned already, Edgar Dubrow was Bigelow's disgraced former veterinarian, and Shelby

Boon's predecessor. With his round wire-rim glasses and beady black eyes, his toothbrush mustache, and his oiled and severely parted hair, Dubrow even *looked* like a Nazi bureaucrat; few people in town were shocked when the *Bugle* exposed him as a closeted Aryan Brother. Mrs. Gowran once told me that watching Dubrow operate on her beloved cat Bootsy was like watching Laurence Olivier take a dentist's drill to Dustin Hoffman's pearly whites in *Marathon Man*. I thought it strange that Dubrow would find sanctuary for *any* jackass; given his political views, especially a *foreign* jackass. Maybe he was trying to atone for his sins.

Grabowski said, "The doc said he'd been performing in shows down in T.J."

"What kinda shows?"

"The doc didn't say. The circus, I guess. Haven't seen him do any tricks, mind."

He could've been a wirewalker, I thought, using his own schlong for a tightrope.

A moth-eaten blanket was draped across the donkey's back.

Written on the blanket was a hand-painted sign:

DONKEY RIDE—$5

I pictured the jackass with a kid riding on his back, walking laps around the yard with his freakish johnson snaking through the dirt in their wake.

"You don't actually take kids for rides on that thing?" I said, appalled.

"They got five bucks, I do. Shit, son. They gotta

learn about the birds n' bees sometime. Now are you quite finished eyeing Enrique's meat? I thought you was here to see the chupacabra?"

6.

Grabowski led me to a tall, dome-shaped cage with a dropcloth draped over it.

A crude illustration of the chupacabra was painted on the cloth, a beast with blazing red eyes and grossly exaggerated fangs and claws.

"As read about in the *Weekly World News*," Grabowski announced, "Mexico's notorious goatsucker . . . I give you—" Grabowski whipped away the cloth like Norman Bates surprising Marian Crane in the shower. "The chupacabra!"

Gizmo started in fright as the sunlight hit him like an interrogator's lamp. He was huddled in the back of the straw-strewn cage. His tail was tucked and his yellow snaggleteeth were chattering with fear. He looked up at me with watery eyes, seemed to recognize me, or maybe my foot, and gave a little yip of relief. He scuttled to the front of the cage and started scratching his claws like a convict raking his mess cup across the bars of his jail cell. The past few days must have been tough on the poor bastard; Grabowski's Gas & Zoo was a long way to fall from his life of luxury as a pampered ex-show dog and stud.

"Careful, son," Grabowski warned me, "don't get too close."

He'd taken the tranq gun from his shoulder and

was pointing it at Gizmo.

I eyed the gun warily, wondering how to break the news to him gently.

"I hate to say it, Mr. Grabowski, but that ain't a chupacabra."

The old man gave a snort of derision. "Says the fella who mistook an orangutan for a skunk ape . . ." But I'd planted a seed of doubt in his mind. "What is it, it ain't a chupacabra?"

"It's a Chinese crested terrier."

"Chine-ee what?"

"It's a dog."

"You expect me to believe that ugly fucking thing is a dog?"

I nodded. "With an owner who misses him terribly."

"Owner? Christ, they'd have to be blind."

Before leaving Harry's office, I'd taken the photo of Harry and his wife and their ugly fucking dog. Covering Harry's face with my thumb—I remembered Harry telling me there was bad blood between him and the old man—I showed the photo to Grabowski. The old man winced at the sight of Mrs. Muffet.

"Jesus wept! That is one severe-looking woman. Who's the lucky hubby?"

He pulled the photo from my hand and suddenly saw who had sent me. "*Muffet.*" Spitting the name like a curse. "Did that cocksucker send you?" He whipped the barrel of the tranq gun towards me. "Send you here to strong-arm me?"

I flashed my palms. "Whoa, hey. Nothing like that. He just didn't want to get the law involved."

"The law?"

"Dognapping is a serious crime."

"Dognap? I didn't dognap shit! I was working in the yard when this ugly sumbitch just sprung outta nowhere, started humping my foot."

I nodded sympathetically. "He does that."

Careful not to make any sudden moves, I slowly raised the leg of my pants to reveal the dog's faded semen stain on my shoe.

Grabowski glanced at a similar stain on his own shoe. "Huh . . ." Realizing I was telling the truth, the old man lowered his gun and kicked the dirt angrily. "Well, goddamn it! I just wasted a week's pension on getting them flyers printed."

"I'm sure Mr. Muffet will compensate you for your trouble."

"By check, I suppose? Maybe he'd like to compensate me for the piece-of-shit truck he sold me too? Cocksucker told me he wasn't responsible once it left the lot. Can you believe that? All the trouble he caused me, I'm tempted to keep his ugly fucking dog."

"Mr. Grabowski, what would that howler monkey say if he knew you were keeping this here dog against his will?"

Grabowski frowned. "Oh, you're a rotten sonofabitch using that against me . . ." He gave a long sigh. "The hell with it. Take the ugly fucking thing. It's been putting the other critters off their feed just to look at him anyway."

He unlocked the cage and opened the rusty gate.

Gizmo sprang from the cage and into my arms, started licking my face. I recoiled from his breath.

"What the hell have you been feeding him?"

Grabowski waited until the dog had slathered my entire face in stinking slobber. Then he gave a wheezy chuckle and said, "Nothing he enjoys eating as much as his own asshole. He's hardly had his tongue outta hisself the whole time he's been here."

Resisting the urge to dropkick the fucking mutt, I yanked Gizmo away from my face. "Thanks for the heads-up."

"Now, I'm gonna need you to sign for him," Grabowski said. "I'm not risking that Muffet cocksucker suing me for disfiguring his dog. He was ugly like this when I found him."

I didn't put that past Harry myself. "Fair enough."

Tucking Gizmo under my arm, I followed Grabowski back inside the store.

7.

Grabowski set the tranq gun down on the counter and searched for a scrap of paper. He found an empty paper peanut sack, and shot an accusing glance at the possum, as if the sack hadn't been empty when he left it. The possum scuttled guiltily through the window behind the counter.

Grabowski was scrawling a receipt on the peanut sack, when an engine roared outside—sounded like Tiberius must've done in his glory days. Then a badass-black Toronado swooped to a stop on the forecourt. It was towing a horsebox trailer. Two men climbed from the car.

The first fella was a wiry young dude with shifty eyes and the downtrodden demeanor of a battered housewife. His mop of blond hair was buzzed to the scalp at the sides and grown into a scraggly rat-tail at the back. He was wearing a flannel shirt with the sleeves ripped off. A loveheart tattoo on his bicep read PROPERTY OF MITCHELL COOGLER. Under the shirt he wore a tight white tee shirt, knotted above his navel like a loose gal's midriff top.

The second guy was a monster. Six-five, and heavyweight, at least, ripped to the bone. With his clean-shaved skull and jet-black mustache, waxed and twisted into curlicues at the tips, he reminded me of an old-time circus strongman, minus the leotard. He wore black leather jeans and a skintight black muscle shirt. His huge muscled arms were sleeved with Aryan Brotherhood and jailhouse ink. The sides of his neck were tattooed with SS lightning bolts like a Nazi Frankenstein's monster. His HGH-bloated gut ballooned over a gleaming chrome death's head belt buckle. I guessed he must be Mitchell Coogler; why he'd brand his name on the little fella, I had no idea, nor did I want to know.

Grabowski saw them and sighed. "I hope they're not here to see the chupacabra."

Somehow I didn't think they were.

FOUR

A FISTFUL OF DONKEY-DONG

1.

Grabowski pushed the peanut sack and pen across the counter towards me.

"Sign that, I'll be right back."

I watched as he shuffled outside to welcome his visitors with his standard greeting: "Grill's broke, I don't got no gas, and the zoo tour's ten bucks."

It was hard not to like the ornery old fart.

The big guy—Coogler—gave a laugh like a rumble of thunder. "We ain't here for no zoo tour, old man." Grabowski bristled in offense. "You got something that belongs to us."

"Take that tone with me," Grabowski said, "you're damn right I got something for you: A foot in your ass. Go on now, git. Before I set the tiger on you."

It was a toothless threat, literally.

But Coogler wasn't to know that, and he just laughed.

These boys had my Spidey sense a-tingling. I thought I'd better head outside and see if Grabowski needed help. The cranky old coot would likely resent my assistance, but things seemed pretty heated out there. But I couldn't just swagger outside with a Chinese crested terrier tucked under my arm. That wasn't going to intimidate anyone—though it might defuse the situation if the big guy and his wiry wingman started laughing at me.

I looked around for somewhere to stash the mutt. Surely Grabowski had an empty box or crate I could use. Best I could find was an empty grain sack. I stuffed Gizmo inside it—which he didn't like much, yipping furiously—knotted the top, and then placed it on the counter next to Grabowski's rifle.

I was about to turn and head outside—

When a shotgun roared, and Grabowski came crashing through the storefront window in a spray of glass and guts. Grabowski's animals, panicked by the shotgun blast, stampeded through the store; the flock of parrots escaped through the shattered window. Grabowski thudded to the floor and skidded to a stop at my feet. Bloody scraps of newspaper were glued to the ragged red hole punched through his torso. His eyes were wide, his teeth bared in pain.

There'd been no howler monkey to warn the old man this time.

In shock, I looked out the shattered window and saw Coogler clutching a stumpy Mossberg pump gun. Wraiths of smoke lassoed from the barrel.

We locked eyes; I'd seen more humanity in the eyes of the beasts in Grabowski's menagerie.

"How's the tour?" he asked me.

Said it so casual I almost replied: *Yeah, pretty good*—

Then he racked the shotgun and fired at me. Instinctively I ducked. The shot sailed over my head. The cash register exploded on the counter. A tickertape parade of shredded banknotes rained down over the store. Coogler racked the shotgun once more. Before he fired again, I turned and vaulted the counter, snatching Gizmo's sack in one hand and Grabowski's rifle in the other, and leaving myself with no hands to cushion my fall.

I slammed the floor face first, performed a clumsy somersault, and crumpled in a heap of pain. Before I'd recovered, Rat-tail stormed inside the store, firing a revolver, potting clutter from the counter that clattered and smashed on the floor all around me. The revolver clicked empty and I heard him curse and then the clink of brass as he fed fresh shells into the cylinder.

Still dazed from face-planting the floor, I teetered up from behind the counter with the rifle in my hands. I squeezed the trigger. The rifle coughed like a peashooter. The dart whistled through the air and buried itself deep in Rat-tail's right eye. His head rocked back and he let out a stuck-pig squeal and started dancing an agonized tarantella. He fumbled for the dart and ripped it from his eye. His eyeball came with it, wrenched from the socket with a ghastly slurping sound, skewered on the dart like an olive on a cocktail stick. Bloody eyeball fluid slopped from the gory hollow. The eye that remained in his skull widened in horror.

Coogler crashed through the door behind him.

"Damn it, Billy. What the hell are you hollering about?"

Rat-tail—aka Billy—thrust his skewered eyeball towards Coogler.

Coogler said, "Jesus."

Then he glanced around the store at the panicked animals.

"Jesus," he said again.

Then the smell must've hit him. "*Jesus!*"

He saw me standing in shock behind the counter.

With a snarl, he racked the shotgun and raised it towards me.

I hurled the empty tranq gun at him, stalling him long enough to grab Gizmo's sack and dive through the open window behind the counter.

2.

I landed with a woof on a crash mat of straw. I was in the five-legged donkey's pen. The jackass didn't like me invading his space, started snorting and stamping his hooves. I patted his flanks, trying to calm him down. Enrique must have got the wrong idea because he turned his head and batted his eyes and gave me what I swear was a coquettish look. Then his johnson started unspooling like an ominous serpent slithering down from a tree, coiling in the dirt between his hind legs. Before I could flee, Coogler burst from the store into the zoo yard. I had no choice but to duck down behind the donkey and try to conceal myself. The little guy came stumbling into the yard in Coogler's wake. "Mitchell . . ." said Billy, in a groggy voice. "I ain't feeling so good, man . . ."

I imagined he wasn't, not with a head full of tiger tranquilizer. Billy could count himself lucky Tiberius was so old, that the cat didn't require a stronger dose of tranquilizer, else he'd have been comatose already.

Billy wobbled and collapsed facedown in the yard and started snoring heavily. Coogler crouched down beside him and checked his pulse, slapped his face but couldn't rouse him. He rolled Billy into the recovery position. Then he climbed back to his feet, racked another round into his shotgun and started sweeping the barrel over the yard. "Mister! You come out now, I'll make it quick."

Well, I wasn't falling for that shit. Hunkered down behind the jackass, I hugged the sack containing Gizmo to my chest, more for my comfort than the dog's. The little fucker nipped me through the sack. I yelped in pain as his snaggly fangs punctured the web of flesh between my thumb and forefinger.

Coogler whirled towards the cry. Seeing me, he grinned, tweezing one end of his circus strongman mustache between his fingers like a vaudeville villain.

"Alright, shitbird. Out from behind that jackass, right now."

I was surprised he didn't just shoot Enrique and me both. He'd just murdered Grabowski in cold blood, and didn't strike me as an animal lover. He approached the donkey pen slowly with his shotgun raised.

Enrique started backing up, snorting and stamping the earth. Afraid to take my eyes off Coogler, I reached out to stop the jackass from kicking me, or crushing me against the back of the pen. I blindly gripped hold of his leg—

It was not his leg.

I let go at once; tried to, at least.

But the strap of my watch had somehow snagged on the loose folds of skin and bristles of the donkey's freakish member, shackling me to him at the wrist. I cried out in horror and jerked my hand back as if from a fire, inadvertently cranking the donkey's dingus like the arm of an old-fashioned slot machine.

Enrique reared onto his hind legs with a heehawing cry. He thrashed his head and whinnied wildly. His reins shook free from the hitching post. And then he shot from the pen like a bullet from a gun. Coogler's eyes widened in shock as Enrique stampeded towards him . . . or maybe it was the sight of me clutching a fistful of donkey-dong as I was dragged through the dirt behind the bolting beast.

Coogler leapt from our path, rolled, came back up with his shotgun raised and his finger on the trigger. As Enrique dragged me past him, I swung the Gizmo-laden sack like a mace and chain, striking the shotgun barrel and throwing off Coogler's aim. The wild blast blew a hole in the fence. A section of sheet metal collapsed like a drawbridge, revealing the filling station forecourt and the highway beyond. Enrique saw the opening and bolted towards it.

I glanced back, saw Coogler rack another round and take careful aim. Enrique and me were dead in his sights. He couldn't miss. But instead of blasting us both to hell, at the last second he fired an angry shot at the heavens. Twice now Coogler had refused to shoot the jackass. *Why?* I wondered. Much as it's possible to think of anything when you're dirt-surfing behind a jackass by its cock.

Enrique bolted through the hole in the fence. Dust billowed in our wake as he tore across the forecourt. To my surprise, Harry was still in the Jeep. I could've kissed the dumb sonofabitch for not running out on me. Then I remembered I'd taken the truck keys. He'd had no choice but to stay. Harry saw me skidding through the dirt behind Enrique, and what I was holding, and his eyes bugged wide and his jaw dropped in shock. Enrique was still wearing that sign on his back: DONKEY RIDE - $5. Maybe Harry thought this was part of the tour?

Harry's head did a slow turn as I was dragged past the truck screaming "Help!"

Then we were thundering away down the highway. I bobbed and moved my head, like I was still in my boxing prime, just to avoid the donkey's storming hooves. The blacktop ripped my shirt and jeans to rags. Scraped my knees and elbows raw. My belt buckle raked the asphalt, spraying sparks in my wake.

I glanced back once more, as much to keep the flying dust from my eyes, and saw Coogler charging through the hole in the fence. We were by now beyond firing range. Coogler bellowed in rage as we galloped away.

He glanced at the Toronado, as if considering a pursuit, but seemed reluctant to abandon Billy, who as far as I knew, remained unconscious in the zoo yard.

Then he spotted Harry cowering in the Jeep. Coogler smashed out the window with the butt of his shotgun, and dragged Harry, screaming, from the cab.

The last thing I saw was Coogler shoving Harry back against the Jeep and jamming the shotgun barrel under his chin—

Then a hoof dashed my skull, and that's all she wrote, I was out.

3.

I came to, facedown in mud, skull pounding like taiko drums, my left arm thrust stiffly before me. Peeling my face from the mud, I regurgitated a mouthful of dirt. My vision blurred into focus. Enrique's hairy ass hovered above my head. Night had fallen. A sliver of moon hung in the sky like a silvery sickle blade. We were in the Sticks someplace. Enrique must've pulled off the highway for a rest stop. His head was bowed to drink from a waterhole. My wrist remained shackled to his johnson; my other hand still clutched the sack containing Gizmo. I didn't know if the dog was dead or alive. I gave the sack a little shake. Gizmo gave a groggy growl. He sounded like I felt.

Releasing my grip on the sack, I clambered gingerly to my knees, reached between Enrique's hind legs, and attempted to unfasten the strap of my watch. It was a delicate operation. I didn't want to goose him, and have him take off again. The watch was snagged on Enrique like a tick. To an outside observer—please god, no one was watching—it would've looked like I was molesting the jackass. After some effort, I managed to loosen the watch-strap and worm my hand free. My deadened arm fell limp by my side. My watch remained dangling from Enrique's johnson like a ticking cock-ring. He could keep it. Under the circumstances, I'm sure Nic Cage would've understood.

I massaged some life back into my arm, hissing as the limb prickled with pins and needles. I was lucky the jackass hadn't wrenched my arm from the socket as he'd dragged me along. Not that I was feeling very lucky just then; quite the opposite. I crawled to the edge of the waterhole, bowed my head alongside Enrique's, and examined my reflection in the murky surface of the water.

I'd seen better days. My forehead was gashed where Enrique had hoofed me. That'd leave a good U-shaped scar. My nose was smeared across my cheek. Fortunately, I'd broken it so many times during my boxing career that the cartilage was malleable as Play-Doh, and I was able to mold it back into an approximate nose shape. I washed my hands—thoroughly—then I cleaned my face and gulped a few scoops of brackish water.

My wits started slowly returning; but that was nothing to brag about.

Memories of my escape from Grabowski's were hazy—being hoofed in the head by a jackass will do that—the last thing I remembered was seeing Coogler drag Harry from the Jeep and shove a shotgun in his face. Considering how ruthlessly Coogler had murdered old Grabowski, it didn't bode well for Harry.

I reached in my pocket for my cellphone and produced a rubble of broken phone parts. Well, so much for palming this clusterfuck onto the law.

With a heavy sigh, I staggered to my feet and tried to get my bearings. Behind me, the undergrowth was trampled flat where Enrique had plowed a path from the highway to the waterhole. I figured the quickest course of action was to ride back to Grabowski's, call the cavalry from there. That's right, I said ride.

I patted Enrique's neck.

"Alright, pard. This time let's try it the old-fashioned way."

Gripping his mane, I hauled myself astride the donkey's back, stifling a hiss of pain as my balls took my weight. It had been many years since I'd ridden, and never bareback, or on a jackass. I slung Gizmo's sack on my shoulder like a hillbilly Santa. Then I tugged Enrique's mane, heeled his ribs, and turned him towards the highway. I spurred him again, Enrique trotted forwards, and away we went.

4.

As we neared the filling station, I reined Enrique to a halt, surveying the scene and trying to decide if I was blundering into an ambush. A small herd of petting zoo animals had escaped through the hole in the fence and were roaming the forecourt. I couldn't see Coogler and Billy anywhere. The black Toronado with the horsebox trailer was gone. My Jeep was still there on the forecourt—what was left of it. The tires were slashed, the hood yawned open, and even from this distance I could see the engine had been shot to shit. I wouldn't be driving out of here, although by now I considered Enrique more reliable and only slightly less comfortable than the damn Wagoneer anyway.

I saw no sign of Harry, dead or alive. Inside the store, maybe?

Reasonably sure that Coogler and Billy weren't hiding in ambush, I giddied Enrique onto the fore-court, climbed down from his back, hitched his rope to the porch rail, left Gizmo's sack on the porch, and then I warily entered the store.

Grabowski's Gas & Zoo had a new attraction: Flies.

Buzzing over Grabowski's corpse like Lilliputians swarming Gulliver.

The old man was sprawled on the floor where he'd crashed through the window. I felt a pang of sorrow for Grabowski; he'd survived firefights in the 'Nam, only to be back-shot by thugs in his own damn zoo. A number of animals were crowded around the corpse like mourners at a wake . . . or maybe diners waiting for the all-you-can-eat buffet to open.

But where was Harry?

It didn't make sense for Coogler to have killed him, and then gone to the trouble of hiding his body, while just leaving Grabowski to rot on the floor; he must have taken Harry with him. What the hell was going on here? I felt hopelessly out of my depth, and I wasn't wearing water wings.

I went behind the store counter and snatched the landline phone from its wall mount. No dial tone. Either Grabowski hadn't paid Ma Bell, or Coogler had cut the phone line. I slammed the phone down, cursing Harry and his ugly fucking dog for getting me into this mess. But I knew I only had myself to blame. I should've left well enough alone, instead of playing hero.

Feeling eyes on me, I glanced back at Grabowski's corpse. A mangy coyote was licking the frozen tears from his face. The sow that'd been snoring on the army rack was now nudging the old man with her snout, as if trying to revive him. The rest of the critters surrounded him like grief-stricken mourners at a chapel of rest. Was it my imagination, or were they staring at me expectantly, as if demanding I avenge their murdered master . . . ? Probably my imagination, yeah.

But I knew I couldn't walk away from this.

Harry might've been an asshole—hell, there was no 'might' about it—but I couldn't just abandon him, and risk him haunting me to my dying days. There was nothing else for it; I'd have to ride back to The Henhouse and call the cops from there.

Before leaving the store, I picked Grabowski off the floor—I didn't trust his critters not to eat him— and laid him in state on the counter. The little possum snuggled beside him like chief mourner, looking genuinely distraught, and I choked down a lump in my throat. I shrouded his corpse with a few tee shirts from the souvenir stand. I could've used one of the shirts myself, to replace the shirt I'd ripped to rags being dragged behind Enrique. Unfortunately Grabowski didn't stock my husky size.

I went back outside to Enrique and Gizmo.

John Wayne once said:

"Courage is being scared to death, but saddling up anyway."

I was scared to death, all right; dealing with a monster like Mitchell Coogler, you bet I was. But as I lowered myself gingerly onto Enrique's back, hissing as my balls were squashed beneath me, I only wished I had a saddle.

FIVE

DONKEY TONK

1.

Enrique trotted to a stop outside The Henhouse. I dismounted stiffly, gave my legs a little shake to coax my balls back down from my abdomen, and then hitched Enrique to the wing mirror of Lou's car. Toting Gizmo's sack on my shoulder, I went inside.

Walt was behind the slab, still experimenting with the recipe for his Skunk Ape cocktail like the Nutty Professor in his lab. "You're late," he said, not looking up.

It wasn't like Walt was rushed off his feet. The place was near most dead, apart from a huddle of college kids in the corner I might've carded, had I been at work on time. Most of the regulars had blown their paychecks, not to mention their loads, at last weekend's *Wet G-String Nite*.

Lou was there, of course.

After heading home to freshen up, he'd reclaimed his spot at the end of the stage, and was waving a buck under Marlene's ass like a loyal courtier fanning his queen's derriere. He gave me a little nod as I entered—my torn and bloody appearance didn't seem to faze him in the slightest—before returning his attention to Marlene.

I collapsed on my stool at the end of the slab.

I said to Walt, "I need a cold beer, change for the phone, my jackass needs water, oh, and here—" I handed him the writhing grain sack: "Put this somewhere safe."

Walt finally noted my appearance, blinked, but didn't comment right away. He peered inside the sack and wrinkled his nose. "The hell are you bringing a rat in my place?"

"It's a dog."

"Say it is?" He took another look. "Ugliest fucking dog I ever saw."

Walt removed Gizmo from the sack, holding the dog at arm's length like he was clutching a baby with a stinky load in his diaper. He didn't seem to know what to do with the mutt. Finally he shoved Gizmo on the back-bar's top shelf, where it was too high for him to jump down. Gizmo scuttled back and forth along the shelf, yipping furiously at Walt. "Screw you, too," Walt said.

Walt looked outside and saw the jackass peering through the window like a horny teenager spying on the gals. "I thought Muffet was gonna give you a truck?"

"It's a long story."

"Well shit, Reggie. You show up late for work on a jackass, with a rat-looking dog in a sack, looking the way you do—more than usual, I mean . . ." He propped his elbow on the bar and leaned towards me. "I wanna hear it."

"Later," I said. "Right now I've gotta call Randy-Ray. Can I get a quarter?"

"Am I gonna get it back?"

"Damn it, Walt!"

Walt opened the register and fished out a quarter. I went to the phone kiosk and called the town stationhouse. Martha Gooch, who doubled as Randy-Ray's secretary, answered the phone. "I'm sorry, Reggie," she said, when I asked to speak to Randy-Ray. "But the Constable's unavailable right now. He's on a stakeout."

"Which steakhouse?"

"StakeOUT," she said. "He's chasing a lead on that—that bucket seller business." For a moment I wondered what she was talking about. In all the excitement, I'd almost forgotten about Randy-Ray's swollen gonads. "He gave me strict instructions he isn't to be disturbed," Martha said. I could hear the guilt in her voice; her eye for a bargain had nearly cost her husband his manhood.

Before I could stress how important it was—

The front door burst open. I heard wild braying and hooves thundering across the floorboards, like some rampaging beast of the apocalypse. I wheeled around inside the kiosk. The phone dropped from my hand in shock. Walt shouted, "Reggie! Get your goddamn jackass outta here!"

Enrique was loose. He'd torn the wing mirror from Lou's car and come galloping inside the bar. He was sheeted in sweat like a racehorse, his upper lip curled in a toothy leer. His eyes were wild, bugging in his skull like a tweaker on a meth binge—and they were locked on Marlene as she twerked her fat ass upon the stage. The donkey's johnson was whipping and writhing like a monstrous black tentacle from an H.P. Lovecraft story. Walt spluttered, "Sweet merciful Jesus!" And then the animal charged headlong at Marlene.

I scrambled from the phone kiosk—too late—Enrique had already raced past me, smashing through tables and chairs as he charged Marlene like an equine stage invader. Marlene saw the donkey coming and screamed. On hands and knees, she scuttled away down the stage, glancing back in terror and colliding headfirst with the dance-pole. A gong-like clang echoed through the bar, and she collapsed out cold on the stage, a fleshy avalanche of woman with her ass heaped invitingly in the air. Enrique rushed forwards to claim his prize.

Lou leapt to his lady's defense. He snatched his sports coat from the back of his chair and started waving it like a matador, yelling at Enrique, "Yah! Get back! Yah!" But Enrique just butted Lou aside and attempted to scale the stage. Rearing onto his hind legs, he hooked his forelegs on the platform, his hooves clattering for purchase on the slippery floor. Unable to drag himself up, he heehawed in frustration. The size of his johnson, I half-expected him to whip his wang around the dance-pole and winch himself onto the stage.

I grabbed the donkey's reins and tried to drag him back. But the beast was freakish strong, and the sight of Marlene's ass had driven him to frenzy. Lou tried to help, but made the mistake of straying behind the donkey and pulling his tail. Enrique jacked his legs and kicked Lou clear the length of the bar. Lou crash-landed on the *Smokey and the Bandit* pinball machine. The glass tabletop shattered and Lou sank down inside the machine like a corpse in a gaudy coffin. The machine teetered under Lou's weight, then the legs gave way and it crashed to the floor. The backboard blew up in a John Woo-explosion of light and sparks. Burt Reynolds's automated laughter wheezed through the room in an electronic death rattle.

Walt racked his shotgun behind me. "Step aside, Reggie."

I stepped between Walt and the jackass. "Wait!"

According to boxing legend, to win a wager, the Panamanian slugger Roberto 'Hands of Stone' Duran once kayoed a horse with a single punch.

But I'm no Duran; it took me a full three-punch combination.

I whaled on the jackass with a left and a right that whipped Enrique's head from side to side, and then I put him to sleep with an uppercut that snapped his snout heavenwards, damn near stretched his neck like a giraffe.

Enrique's legs buckled, his ears twitched, and then he keeled on his side with a heehawing moan, his johnson wilting across the floor like a fire hose.

2.

"Goddamn," Walt said, lowering the shotgun.

"Now I didn't want to do that," I said. "Anyone asks—PETA, anyone—it was self-defense."

"*Goddamn,*" Walt said again.

I helped free Lou from the guts of the pinball machine. It was damaged beyond repair. So much for earning my high score back. I could have cried.

Marlene snorted awake like a walrus from a nightmare. "What happened?" she said, propping herself against the dented dance-pole.

I clapped Lou on the back. "Lou here defended your honor."

"He—he did?"

Lou shot me a grateful glance.

"Wasn't nothing," he said to Marlene. "Any man would've done the same."

Marlene reached down from the stage, snatched Lou's tie and yanked him towards her, and planted a big smackeroo on his head. "My hero."

Lou flushed redder than the sucker-print of lipstick on his scalp.

Marlene peered down nervously at the unconscious jackass.

"Is—is it dead?"

"I don't know," I said. "Lou hit him pretty hard."

Lou gave me a look like I was overdoing it now.

We crowded around the out-cold jackass. Walt prodded Enrique's side with his shotgun barrel, got no response, and then teased the donkey's mane from his face.

Lou let out a gasp. "It—it can't be."

I said, "Friend of yours?"

"You mean to say you don't recognize him? Fellas, this right here is Enrique."

I shrugged.

Lou said, "Otherwise known as 'Mister Head.'"

Walt frowned. "Wasn't Mister Ed a horse?"

I said, "Of course, of course."

Walt snickered.

"Not Mister Ed," Lou said. "Mister *Head*."

Walt and me exchanged blank looks. Lou rolled his eyes, apparently convinced we were just acting coy. "Oh, c'mon now, boys! *Enrique!* He's only the most celebrated adult entertainment animal of his generation!"

Walt said to me, "The jackass didn't kick Lou in the head, did he?"

Lou explained—with nerdish enthusiasm—that *Mister Head* was a popular porn parody series. A riff on the old TV show, it chronicled the sexcapades of the freakishly endowed, dirty-talking donkey as he cuckolded and cock-blocked his hapless human owner, Wilbur.

Walt said, "Jesus, Lou! How do you know this stuff? Didn't you used to teach Sunday school?"

But Lou wasn't finished: "When Enrique's adult entertainment career petered out—no pun intended—his owners sold him to a Mexican bordello to see out his twilight years as the star of a donkey show."

I said, "Beats the glue factory, I guess."

"It was like seeing Marlon Brando reduced to dinner theater." Lou gazed down in awe at the unconscious jackass. "What in the world is Mister Head doing in Bigelow?"

"More to the point," Walt said, "what's he doing on my floor?"

That's when everyone looked at me.

So I told them everything that had happened—from Harry recruiting me to retrieve his Chinese crested terrier after it was mistaken for a chupacabra . . . to my escape by donkey-cock from Grabowski's Gas & Zoo.

When I was finished, Walt shook his head slowly.

"You've outdone yourself this time, Levine."

Enrique heehawed back to consciousness. We all started in surprise, backing away as the donkey brayed in pain. Marlene clamped her hands over her ears. "Make it stop, oh god, make it stop!" Walt shouted to me, "What's wrong with him? You think you broke his jaw when you punched him out?"

I crouched down beside Enrique, patted his neck and made soothing noises.

"Who'd you think you are," Walt said, "the Jackass Whisperer?"

The donkey's hide was hot and feverish, slick with sweat. He made a pitiful attempt to right himself, his legs flailing weak as a newborn foal. His eyes rolled up in his skull. He looked at me plaintively to ease his suffering—or maybe he was worried I'd slug him again. Then he thrashed his tail and cut a long foghorn of gas, emitting a hiss of hot air like a slashed tractor tire. Walt, who'd been standing behind him, still basking in his Jackass Whisperer wisecrack, gave a cry of disgust and moved upwind.

"I think—he's got some kind of bellyache," I said. I could sympathize; wasn't long ago I'd had a similar complaint, caused by the ill-advised ingestion of a microwave burrito.

"No shit," Walt said, gagging at the stench.

Enrique was splayed on his side, grinding his teeth as he released a series of strained, high-pitched farts, like gassy Morse code. The white ruff of his belly was grossly distended. I gently parted the fur and found a line of crude, inflamed sutures, zigzagging his abdomen like a rusted zipper on a 1950s movie monster. Five rectangular shapes bulged against his swollen gut. They were roughly the same shape and size as television remote controls. I tried to imagine the jackass devouring a whole TV remote, and liking the taste so much that he ate another four; it seemed unlikely. I lightly prodded one of the shapes. Enrique heehawed in pain and cut another long fart. "Stop that!" Walt said. "I'll be airing this place for a damn month."

"There's something inside him," I said. "He's like a living piñata."

"Maybe it's aliens," Marlene said.

Walt and me looked at her.

"I seen it on *The Unexplained Files*," she said, "how the aliens in-semen-ate people n' stuff." Marlene had experience of alien insemination; she'd birthed two bastards by illegal day laborers. "You oughta kill it now, Walt. Shoot it in the head and set it on fire before it hatches donkey aliens."

"We'll file 'aliens' under the maybe column, Marlene," I told her.

I returned my attention to Enrique, and the strange rectangular shapes bulging against his belly.

Walt said, "What're you thinking, Reggie?"

I was thinking: *Why does this shit keep happening to me?*

What I said was: "Damned if I know what's going on here . . ."

I glanced at the phone kiosk. "But I know someone who might."

"Who?" Walt said, as I went and made the call. "Doctor Dolittle?"

3.

The cavalry arrived within the hour. I was waiting outside, necking a couple few Coors to settle my nerves. I'd used the bar's first aid kit to clean and dress my grazes, stuck Band-Aids over my cuts, and the gash in my forehead, till my mug resembled a crudely repaired clay vase. I'd also changed out of the tee shirt I'd ripped to rags while being dragged behind Enrique, and donned a rumpled Hawaiian shirt, adorned with palm trees and toucans, from the lost and found crate in the stockroom. I just had to hope that slashed jeans were still hip.

Shelby's truck pulled up outside, and my stomach butterflied, and I drained the dregs of my beer and hid the bottle with the other empties. Shelby climbed from the truck, carrying a Gladstone medicine bag.

She was mad as a wasp. Her eyes were all puffy and red and her hair was ironed flat on one side where she'd been sleeping on it. She was wearing tossed-on civvies of a jersey and jeans. But to me, she still looked a million dollars. I said, "Thanks for coming, Doc—"

"Mr. Levine!" she said, the way the teachers in school used to call on me in class when I was wool-gathering. "Do you have any idea what time it is?"

As a matter of fact, I didn't. Enrique was no longer wearing my watch as a cock-ring. I assumed it must have fallen loose and been lost when we were riding to The Henhouse. I decided not to share this with Shelby. I said, "It's late, I guess."

"This had better be important like you said on the phone," she said. "I don't appreciate being dragged from bed in the middle of the night and brought to a place like . . . *this*."

She looked up at The Henhouse and shuddered.

"It really ain't as bad as you think, Doc."

Come to think of it, it was probably worse.

"What's so important it couldn't wait until office hours, Mr. Levine?"

"Reggie," I insisted. "How many times I gotta ask you to call me Reggie?"

"I'd prefer to keep things formal."

"I understand. You're on duty."

"In general."

"Gotcha . . . Well, like I said on the phone, it's kinda hard to explain."

"Then maybe I should just see for myself—"

She moved towards the door and I blocked her path like I was carding her.

"Doc, wait. I oughta warn you. It ain't pretty in there."

"Mr. Levine," she said, with a condescending smile. "Before starting my surgery in Bigelow, I served two tours with *Veterinaires sans Frontieres*."

I nodded like I had a clue what she was talking about.

"Veterinarians Without Borders," she explained. "I can assure you, there is nothing inside this fine establishment that can shock me. Except maybe the clientele."

She gestured for me to move out of her way. "Now, please. The sooner I get this over and done with—*whatever* the big mystery is—the sooner I can go back to bed. I have a surgery first thing in the morning."

So I opened the door and held it open, which she seemed to resent—a fella can't even be a gentleman anymore. She brushed past me, but hadn't taken two steps inside before stopping dead in her tracks.

Enrique was lying on his side on the pool table. Don't ask me how we got him up there: Wasn't easy. Lou was busy tucking Enrique's johnson into the left corner pocket, out of harm's way. Marlene was just standing there in her G-string and pasties, looking worried the jackass was about to spawn alien-donkey hybrids. Walt was plying the nag with whiskey poured through a funnel.

Shelby sputtered in disbelief, "What the hell are you—are you giving that animal *alcohol*?"

"Thought I'd save you the trouble and anesthetize him," Walt said. "Don't worry, Doc. He seems to like it. As well he might. It's the good stuff."

It figured Walt would save the good stuff for a jackass.

Enrique smacked his lips and puckered up ready for another shot.

Walt chuckled dotingly and poured another measure down the funnel.

"Stop!" Shelby said. "That's enough!"

Walt removed the funnel from Enrique's mouth. "Sorry, bud. Veterinarian's orders."

Shelby took a deep breath to compose herself. She set her medicine bag on the corner of the pool table and was about to start examining her patient. Then she noticed the Chinese crested terrier scuttling back and forth along the top shelf behind the bar, yipping furiously. "Would someone please shut that dog up?"

That's years of veterinary college for you; she recognized the ugly fucking mutt for what it was right away.

"With pleasure," Walt said. "Reggie, where's the duct tape?"

"Just put him in the stockroom," I said.

Walt clearly preferred his idea, but he hiked Gizmo down from the shelf and put him in the stockroom. The dog clawed at the door and yip-yip-yipped.

As Shelby continued her examination of Enrique, teasing her fingers across his swollen belly, and those strange TV-remote-shaped bulges, I wished I was a donkey, instead of a regular jackass. Enrique's eyes rolled drunkenly towards her. Liking what he saw, he gave a lusty sigh, and Lou had to cram his johnson back down inside the corner pocket of the pool table. But thanks to Walt's generosity with the whiskey he was too shitfaced to be any real threat.

Shelby finished her exam, looking grave.

"Someone has sewn something inside this animal."

She looked at me accusingly.

"Hell, Doc. It wasn't none of us. He was like this when I found him."

"And where might that have been?"

"The roadside zoo out on old highway 9."

"Grabowski's," she said, with a knowing sigh.

"You know the place?"

She nodded like she wished she didn't.

"The old man means well, I suppose. But he's a hoarder."

"I noticed."

She looked down at the donkey and stroked his mane; again, I couldn't help feeling a pang of jealousy.

"So—you rescued him?" She sounded surprised; apparently this didn't jibe with what she'd heard about me being the terror of all wildlife.

"Matter of fact," I said, "he rescued me."

Walt said, "Tell the Doc how you escaped from Grabowski's by holding onto his—"

I cut him off quick. "Thank you, Walt! The doc doesn't wanna hear about that."

Before I could give Shelby a sanitized account of what had happened at Grabowski's, Lou stepped forwards: "What's the diagnosis, Doc? No bushwa now. Is Enrique gonna make it?"

"Not unless I operate right away."

Lou choked down a cry. "Don't let him die, Doc! Please! You gotta treat this jackass like he's the President of the United States!" I ushered Lou away before he started telling Shelby about Enrique's dubious celebrity. "Give the doc room to work, Lou." Marlene took Lou off my hands. I nodded thanks to her. The wily old lech pretended he was sobbing and buried his face in her cleavage.

I said to Shelby, "You want us to carry him out to your truck?"

"There's no time for that. I'm going to have to operate right here."

"On my pool table?" Walt said. "Now wait a fucking—"

"Mr. Levine," Shelby said. "I'll need you to assist."

"Assist—like—dab the sweat off your face with a towel or something?"

Shelby smiled at me; the first time she'd ever really smiled at me, and I didn't like it, not one bit. "I'm afraid you'll be getting your hands a little dirtier than that."

Walt shut up about his pool table and grinned. "Oh, this oughta be good."

4.

Shelby disinfected her hands and pulled on latex gloves. She took what she needed to operate from her medicine bag, placing everything neatly on a bar towel she'd unfurled across the pool table. "I need a razor," she said.

Walt returned moments later with his electric razor. "Best I can do."

Shelby buzzed Enrique's belly and then gave him

the local. The needle punctured his swollen belly with a sound like punch pliers popping through leather. Feeling queasy already, I turned my head and closed my eyes and sucked deep breaths. "Exactly what am I doing here, Doc?"

"Just stay where you are, Mr. Levine." She began making the incision, slitting the donkey's belly along the line of the sutures. The scalpel popped through the stitches, sounding like a carpet knife slicing slowly through a thick rug. "Hold this," Shelby said, and though my eyes were closed, I could hear the smug smile in her voice.

Then she slapped something squishy and wet in my hand. Warm liquid oozed through my fingers and spattered onto the felt top of the pool table. I shuddered and choked down my gorge. I heard Walt chuckle. "Y'alright there, Reggie? Looking a little green, son." His voice grew distant, floating away above me like a helium balloon; like Harry Muffet's giant inflatable effigy breaking free from its moorings and drifting silently across town.

And that's about all I remember of the operation, because down I went.

I came around about a half-hour later, still lying flat-out on the floor. People were moving around me like I was a piece of furniture. *Fucking Walt* . . . I bet he hadn't even tried to sit me up. I could hear Enrique snoring on the pool table above me. Then Marlene stepped over me, her ass looming into view like a flabby Death Star. She was still wearing nothing but her G-string and pasties, and was holding up an IV-bag that was hooked to the donkey.

Shelby was cleaning her instruments. She glanced down at me and smirked.

"Aren't you a little squeamish for a boxer?"

"How's the jackass?" I croaked.

"Stable. Considering what he's been through, it's a miracle he survived."

"A miracle, amen," Lou agreed enthusiastically. "Praise God!"

Shelby frowned at Enrique. "I'm still concerned about this bruising on his face—"

I clutched the edge of the pool table and hauled myself to my feet. "He fell on his face when he keeled over," I told Shelby. "Right, guys?"

I shot Walt a shitty look for not rolling me into the recovery position when I passed out, or at least sliding a pillow under my head, but he was staring gravely at something on the edge of the pool table. I figured he was estimating how much it'd cost him to replace the felt tabletop, or if he could get away with leaving it stained with donkey blood.

Then I saw the five plastic-wrapped bricks of white powder.

"That was inside him?"

"Sewn under his hide," Shelby said.

Walt looked at me and said, "It's primo *yayo*, Reggie."

His eyes were big as saucers, near most bursting from his skull.

"And how would you know that?" I said, with a sinking feeling.

Shelby said, "Against my advice, Mr. Wiley insisted on cutting into one of the bags with his pocket knife, and sampling the contents."

"It was the only way to know for sure, Doc," Walt insisted.

"Damn it, Walt," I said. "You promised me you were never gonna touch this shit again." Walt's history of substance abuse is a story for another time, but if you've ever seen *The French Connection II*, the scene where Gene Hackman goes cold turkey should give you an idea of what we went through.

Walt looked away guiltily, swiping his nose and grinding his teeth.

I gazed down at Enrique and the bricks of white powder on the pool table.

"Well, I'll be . . . The damn donkey's a drug mule."

Walt said, "Gotta be about a hundred K's worth here. Maybe more."

"Mr. Levine," Shelby said, "I think you'd better tell me exactly what's going on here."

But before I could, the phone in the phone kiosk started ringing.

Lou went and answered it. "Reggie, it's for you."

"Take a message."

"It's Nicolas Cage again. He sounds real upset."

"Nicolas Cage?" Shelby said.

"Close friend of mine," Walt said, directing her attention to the signed poster behind the bar.

I raced to the kiosk, snatched the phone from Lou.

"Harry!"

I never would've believed I could be so happy to hear his voice.

"Reggie! You gotta help me, man! These fucking guys are crazy—"

The phone was wrenched from his hand. I heard a meaty thud; Harry yelped in pain and started sobbing. Then the devil's baritone of Mitchell Coogler growled down the line: "You got something that belongs to me, motherfucker."

5.

I cut a nervous glance at the jackass convalescing on the pool table, and the bloody bricks of coke Shelby had removed from his gut.

"I'd be happy to return it," I said.

"Mighty white of you," Coogler said.

He took his mouth away from the phone. "Good news, Harry—Hey!" Another thump; another yelp of pain. "I said, good news. Your buddy's gonna bring me back my jackass." He came back on the line. "He's crying he's so happy."

But it didn't sound like tears of joy I could hear in the background. "You don't have to hurt him, man."

"Hard not to," Coogler said. "He's got one of those faces, you know."

"I'll give you what you want. No one else needs to get hurt."

"Like the old man? I feel terrible about that. Like, boo-fucking-hoo. If the stubborn old fuck'd just given me my jackass like I told him, then maybe I wouldn't have had to—"

"Shoot him in the back?" I said with a surge of anger.

Coogler snorted contemptuously. "I'm sorry you had to witness such an ugly scene."

"Me too."

"Have you tattletaled to the law already?"

"No." I neglected to mention that it wasn't for lack of trying.

"Good. Then let's keep this between us girls," Coogler said. "Now get your ass out to Harry's Wherever-the-fuck. Car dealership. Looks like a bomb hit a junkyard."

"I know the place."

"Then it shouldn't take you longer than an hour to get here," he said. "You bring me my jackass, I give you yours."

"There's just one problem."

"Harry's gonna be real sorry to hear that."

"The jackass, he—well, he got sick—something he ate, maybe."

I heard the crunch of plastic as Coogler tightened his fist around the phone.

"I had to call the vet," I told him.

A chill traveled down the phone line; it suddenly felt like I was clutching an icicle to my ear. "What the fuck are you saying to me, punk?"

"I have what you want," I said, "only—it ain't inside the jackass anymore."

"Is it damaged?"

"No."

"All five intact?"

"Yeah."

I heard him exhale.

"Okay. Then I guess you won't need a full hour

after all, not without a jackass to wrangle. Thirty minutes. Come alone. Every minute you're late, there'll be a little less of Harry here waiting for you. Are you feeling me, chief?"

"I understand."

"I hope you do . . .

"And Harry," Coogler said, "he's praying on it."

6.

I hung up the phone and staggered from the kiosk on rubbery legs. Helped myself to a hit of the good stuff Walt had left on the bar slab. Walt opened his mouth to object, closed it again, and mentally deducted what I drank from my next paycheck. I wondered how he'd settle things with Enrique; maybe he could put the donkey to work, have him plow a few yards until the debt was squared.

"The big guy's got Muffet," I said. "Says he'll kill him, he doesn't get his *yayo* back." I prayed Walt hadn't sampled too much of the wares.

"Big guy?" Shelby said, frowning. "Are we still talking about Nicolas Cage?"

I gave a weary laugh and then told her what was going on: "It all started with a chupacabra . . ."

To her credit, Shelby heard me out. Then she shook her head as if to unscramble what I'd told her. "This is some kind of joke, right?" She looked at each of us in turn, even shot a fishy glance at Enrique, as if she suspected the jackass was in on the gag too. "You're making fun of the townie, is that it?"

"I wish it was and I wish we were, Doc."

"This town, I swear . . ." She gave a *give-me-strength* sigh.

"Old man Grabowski," she said, "he's really dead?"

"The big guy—Coogler—he shot him in the back like it was nothing."

Her eyes fired with fury. I made a mental note to never get on her bad side.

Walt said, "What are you gonna do, Reggie?"

I noticed he didn't say 'we.'

"Don't see what other choice I got," I said. "I'm gonna do what Coogler says."

I started bundling the bricks of coke into the same grain sack I'd used to carry Gizmo. The hole Walt had cut in one of the bags, I patched with duct tape.

"This is crazy," Shelby said. "You have to call the police."

"There's no time for that," I said. "And Coogler said no cops, else he'll start carving Muffet up."

"Besides," Walt said. "Reggie's persona non grata with Sheriff Jaynes after that Backseat Strangler thing. The Strangler's lawyer says Reggie used excessive force making his citizen's arrest, reckons he can get the charges dropped. The Sheriff's kinda salty about it. So you can forget about the cavalry riding to the rescue."

"What about Constable Gooch?" Shelby said.

"You didn't hear about his balls?" Walt said.

"And I don't want to."

Shelby looked me up and down like she was trying to picture me as a hero.

"But—but you're just a strip club bouncer, for

God's sake!"

"Thanks for the vote of confidence, Doc," I said. "But I don't see no one else stepping up."

Shelby glanced at Walt.

He promptly snatched Enrique's IV-bag from Marlene. "Hey, I'm nursing the jackass here."

Shelby looked me hard in the eye. "We'll take my truck."

"We?"

She hurriedly packed her supplies back in her medicine bag. "Someone may need medical attention."

"My money's on Reggie," Walt said.

"And you're in no fit state to drive," Shelby added.

I glanced down at myself. "It's just a few bumps and bruises, is all."

"You're drunk, is what I meant."

"*Half*-drunk," I said. "I wasn't, you think I'd be doing this?"

She finished packing her medicine bag and stared me down.

I said, "You sure about this, Doc? These boys; they're some serious bad news hombres." Point of fact, what the fuck was I thinking here?

"You can try and talk me out of it while we're driving," Shelby said.

"Fair enough."

She reached under the back of her jersey and snatched a pistol from a waistband holster. "Whoa!" we all said. Shelby shrugged. "You didn't seriously think I'd come unarmed to a place like this after midnight?" She checked the pistol and returned it to the holster. Walt said, "A place like *what*?"

He returned the IV-bag to Marlene, went behind the bar and reached under the slab, pulled up a shotgun and tossed it to me. "I want this one back."

The last shotgun he loaned me, I'd lost in a firefight with those Damn Dirty Apes.

"I'll do my best."

I gave him a nod and he nodded back; it's a guy thing.

"Soon as we're gone," I said to Walt, "call Martha Gooch back, get through to Randy-Ray, try and convince him this is bigger than his balls."

Walt whistled through his teeth. "I'll try."

I glanced around The Henhouse as if for the last time; I wouldn't be missing much, but I'd miss it all the same.

I slung the sack of coke over one shoulder, propped Walt's shotgun against the other. Walt said, "What about Muffet's ugly fucking dog?"

And just like that, he'd given me a plan. Admittedly it wasn't much of a plan. But even a dumbass plan was better than no plan at all. "Walt, I could kiss you!"

"The hell you will."

Walt fetched Gizmo from the stockroom, and I tucked the dog under my arm and went outside to Shelby's truck, where she was gunning the engine impatiently.

She glanced at Gizmo. "Do I even want to know?"

"Probably not."

Shelby left it at that; she hit the go-pedal and the truck lurched forward and we roared away . . .

Into the night, and to almost certain death.

SIX

TESTICULAR FORTITUDE

1.

For Constable Randy-Ray Gooch, the whole she-bang started with a tingling sensation around the perineum, and the underside of his scrotum. It was not, at first, an entirely unpleasant sensation. A little like when he was setting a new personal best on his exercise bike, and his balls started prickling with pins-and-needles. But then the tingling turned to a rampant jailhouse itch, and there was nothing pleasant about that. No, sir. No amount of scratching could satisfy the itch. And by God, it was not for want of trying; he could hardly keep his hands out of his uniform pants. Soon, he was tearing out pubes by the fistful, like a frantic dog with the mange. Anything to get more purchase on his inflamed nutsack. Frankly it was a poor example to be setting around town.

Hard to lay down the law with your hand down your pants. Pulling over some gal for a traffic violation, he'd felt like Harvey Keitel in the *Bad Lieutenant*, forcing female drivers into lewd displays while he mauled his meat.

Then the swelling started. Like any man in his situation, the first thing he did was ignore it, and pray it went away. Day four of the problem, he emerged from the shower, dropped the towel from around his waist, and said to Martha, "You notice anything different, hon?" His cock looked like a pitiful pale snake that'd choked to death while swallowing a hippity-hop. His balls had swollen to the size of grapefruits. They were cobwebbed with livid purple veins, and seemed to be visibly pulsating. And by now his pubic hair had molted entirely, which really dropped the curtain on the horror show. Martha Gooch screamed and fainted dead away on the bathroom floor.

When she'd recovered, under interrogation from her husband, Martha broke down and tearfully confessed to buying a batch of bootleg laundry detergent from a bucket seller. First wash, she'd used it to clean Randy-Ray's jockey shorts. And in Martha's defense, those shorts had come out dazzling whiter than white. "Damn you, woman!" said Randy-Ray. "I give you a plenty fair allowance. Your eye for a bargain may just cost me my manhood."

Reluctantly he went and saw his doctor. Dropped his drawers, saying: "Now it's probably nothing—" The doctor had him rushed by lights-and-siren ambulance to the hospital emergency ward.

And that's where I met him, shortly after the Backseat Strangler thing, and he told me all about it while I was doped to the gills on painkillers, and a captive audience—so if you think I've told you more than you wanted to hear about Randy-Ray Gooch's privates, well, I sympathize.

After treatment, the swelling went down some—deflating from the size of grapefruits, to baseballs—and he was discharged from hospital and returned to work. To hammock his tender testicles, the doctors had given him the truss to wear under his uniform pants; the bandage mankini I've previously, and would hope *memorably* described. His balls remained bald as Yul Brynner. Randy-Ray was convinced the problem was psychological; that he would not sprout a single pubic hair until he'd brought the bucket selling sonofabitch to justice.

So he started kicking down doors.

Gingerly.

Rounding up the usual town ne'er do wells, he put the squeeze on them until he got an address. According to Gooch's intel, the bucket seller was operating out of the old train yard, having converted an abandoned cattle car into his makeshift laboratory. He staked out the place over several nights, huddled in his unmarked Bronco with an icepack nestled against his nuts. And around the time I was riding Enrique to The Henhouse, Gooch had caught his sworn enemy in the act.

The bucket seller, wearing an army surplus gas mask, was mixing a fresh batch of laundry detergent in an old clawfoot bathtub, stirring the seething witch's brew with a canoe oar. His cattle car laboratory was cluttered with a dozen or more heavy-duty plastic drums, plus the stockpiled chemicals required to manufacture his counterfeit Tide. As Randy-Ray stormed the lab, the bucket seller's eyes widened in surprise through the plastic window of his gas mask.

"Drop the oar! Lemme see those hands!" Randy-Ray yelled at him, his service revolver shaking in his fist. Gooch would later wonder how he'd resisted the urge to just blow the punk away and plant a throwdown piece on him.

The bucket seller did as Randy-Ray told him. Gooch shoved him back roughly against the wall of the cattle car. Clawing the gas mask from his face, Gooch identified the punk as a two-bit yokel wastrel named Dougie Pruitt.

"You fucked up good this time, Pruitt," Gooch said. "You should've stuck to cooking crank like your momma. You're in the big leagues now, son."

Then he groined the sonofabitch with a savage jack of his knee.

Pruitt crumpled to the ground, wheezing in agony.

"And that's just for starters," Gooch promised him.

Gooch gave the punk a little time to recover, relishing his pain. Then he ordered him to start loading the drums of detergent from the cattle car and into the bed of his Bronco truck. And that's what was happening when Martha Gooch patched Walt's call through to the radio mike in the Bronco.

"Damn it," Gooch said, "I told that woman I was

not to be disturbed. What's the big emergency, Walt? You got a phony ID needs my immediate attention?"

"It's a little more serious than that, Randy-Ray."

"Yeah? Tell that to my balls."

Walt told Randy-Ray the whole sorry story; at least, Walt hoped he was speaking to Gooch, and that Randy-Ray wasn't literally holding the radio mike to his crotch.

When Walt had finished, Gooch was silent for several long seconds.

Finally he said, "Run that past me again."

"What part?"

"The part where Reggie's hanging hold of a donkey's cock."

"I know how it sounds, Randy-Ray."

"Nope, I don't think you do." Gooch said, "So let me get this straight . . .

"Old man Grabowski's dead, and the fellas what done it, they're holding Harry Muffet hostage at his car dealership, say they'll kill him if they don't get back the drugs that they smuggled inside a sex mule."

"Donkey," Walt said.

"I stand corrected."

"But that's about the size of it, yeah. Fucking Reggie, huh?"

"Yeah, fucking Reggie . . ." Buoyed, no doubt, by the capture of his nemesis, Gooch announced, "Alright. Here it is. Walt, you and Reggie can breathe a big of sigh of relief, because the lawman's back in town and he's on his fucking way."

2.

Shelby floored the truck through town towards Harry's Pre-Owned American Auto. Riding bitch, I emptied Shelby's Gladstone medicine bag and replaced her tools with the bricks of coke from the grain sack. Gizmo was down in the footwell, nuzzling my ankles like he was trying to decide which foot to start humping first. His ordeal had done nothing to dull his libido. Maybe I was wearing provocative socks? Before his foreplay went any further, I fetched him from the footwell—he gave a thwarted *yip!*—and put him in the medicine bag on top of the coke. He bared his snaggleteeth and snarled at me. I shoved his head down inside the bag and snapped the clasp shut. His muffled yipping echoed from inside the bag.

Shelby gnawed her bottom lip. "This goes against all my principles."

"He'll be fine," I assured her. "By now he's probably getting used to it."

And as if on cue, the dog stopped yipping. "See?"

But I could tell she still wasn't sure.

"You know you don't gotta do this, Doc. You could just drop me off."

My heart skipped a beat as she actually considered my token gesture.

Then she shook her head. "And have your death on my conscience?"

I grinned at her. "Hell, there's no sense in us both dying."

"Let's leave the pep talk there, shall we, Levine?"

She'd dropped the 'Mister.' I called that making progress.

"You looked pretty handy with that pistola back there," I said. "Is that something they taught you at—what'd you call it—Vets Without Borders?"

I wasn't about to embarrass myself by attempting to say it in French.

"Something like that."

"What is that exactly?"

"You've heard of Doctors Without Borders?"

"Of course," I lied. What can I say? I read *Ring* magazine, not *Newsweek*.

"Well, it's similar."

That left me none the wiser; fortunately she clued me in.

"We were stationed at a village in Kenya—"

"Africa," I blurted out.

Like a fucking idiot.

As if to a child, she said: "Kenya's in Africa, that's right."

I needed to claw this one back. "They gotta lotta pets out there, huh."

"They're starving, Levine. We were helping farmers raise sustainable livestock."

I decided to keep my fucking mouth shut.

"One day, we received word a motorist was stranded on the plains. My team leader and I went out there with gas and tools, and a gun, because you never knew. It turned out the 'motorist' was an ivory poacher. His 4x4 had crapped out under the weight of the load he was carrying. The back of the truck was piled high with bloodstained elephant tusks, some of them hacked out of babies, no bigger than walking canes.

"The sonofabitch knew who we were, and that it wasn't in our remit to do a damn thing to stop him. He leered at me like I imagine the men at your club leer at the dancing girls, and said: 'Have I died and gone to heaven?'

"Not quite. I laid into him with the butt of my pistol. By the time my team leader dragged me off, I'd knocked out nearly all of the bastard's teeth."

She sounded like she regretted having missed a few.

I said to Shelby, "Poached a little ivory your own-self, huh?"

That earned me my first genuine Shelby smile. It was so beautiful, I almost forgot about Coogler waiting for me in Harry's rusting automobile graveyard.

"By mutual consent," Shelby said, "it was decided I should come home to the States." She paused. In a softer voice, said: "We didn't do a damn bit of good out there."

"Well . . ." I said, "maybe we can do some good tonight."

Shelby gave me a steely nod.

Then she glanced at the literal doggy bag in my lap, frowned, and continued driving in silence.

3.

Arriving at the dealership, Shelby pulled the truck through the front gate, and we proceeded at a crawl towards Harry's office at the back of the lot. On either side of the wide central lane were banks of used-cars. On every car windshield was a sales sticker with a smugly smiling caricature of Harry. A battalion of smirking Muffets watched as we continued towards the Airstream trailer. The web of tacky plastic pennants, roped above the lot, rasped eerily in the wind like playing cards in cycle spokes. Moored to the roof of the trailer, the balloon Harry loomed above us like an inflatable giant, slowly nodding his head in the breeze. The only light came from Shelby's headlights, and the gleaming guillotine of the waxing moon in the starry night sky.

Coogler and Billy were waiting for us on the court outside the trailer. I should've known better than to hope Billy would still be comatose. The black Toronado was tucked alongside the trailer. The horsebox had been removed from the back of it. Coogler and Billy didn't need it anymore. They hadn't wanted Enrique, only what was inside him.

"What's wrong with the little guy?" Shelby asked me.

"Oh, I shot Billy in the eye with a tranq gun loaded for tiger." She looked like she regretted asking. "It was after they'd killed Grabowski. Self-defense, Doc. Scout's honor."

We climbed from the truck. I left the medicine bag on my seat, praying Gizmo wouldn't start yipping and give the game away. I propped Walt's shotgun in the footwell, and then stood near the open door where it was within easy reach.

Billy was clutching his revolver by his side, giving

me the hairy eyeball with the eye he still had left in his skull. A crude cotton patch covered his right eye. The right side of his face, where I'd shot him with the tranq gun, was drooping as if he'd suffered a stroke. A rope of drool dangled from his twisted lips. His right arm was gimped, the hand a gnarled claw.

Looming beside Billy, Coogler had his stumpy shotgun threaded through the front of his belt. The chrome death's head belt buckle grinned above his crotch. He was holding a lighted road flare in his fist, spewing smoke and red sparks as he waved it about like a kid with a sparkler.

A few paces from Coogler, Harry stood imprisoned within a tower of tires that were stacked from his feet to his chin, the cream filling in a Swiss roll. Empty jerry cans lay around the base of the tires. Harry and the tires had been drenched with gasoline. Fuel pooled around him like a flammable moat.

Harry's face was battered and swollen. His mustache was matted with so much blood it looked like a giant scab above his lip. A cotton patch covered his right eye, matching Billy's; it was as if they were starting some strange new fashion movement. Coogler and Billy—the sonsofbitches—must've gotten Old Testament on the poor bastard, took an eye for an eye.

Harry saw me and started sobbing. He was just about the sorriest sight I'd ever seen in my life. With a surge of anger, I said to Coogler: "What the hell, man! We're here ahead of time. You said you wouldn't hurt him."

"I don't remember saying that," Coogler said. "I do recall telling you to come alone." His eyes flicked to Shelby. "Who's the cunt?"

To her credit, she didn't flinch. "I'm a doctor," she said. "Does anyone need medical attention?"

Billy motioned with his clawed hand to the palsied right side of his face.

"Wugga fugga dink?" he slurred, saliva slopping from the side of his mouth.

I glanced at Coogler. "What was that?"

"Damned if I know," Coogler said. "I'm still getting used to it."

Billy took a deep breath and tried again.

"What. Do. You. Fuck. Ing. Think?"

Shelby took a step towards him. "I could take a look—"

"Uh-uh!" Coogler said. "Let's just everyone stay where they are for now."

I said, "How about you, Harry? You okay?"

Harry sobbed, "They scooped out my eye with a fucking coffee spoon!"

Coogler winced at Harry's shrill voice. "Kinda wish we'd taken his tongue."

Then he said to me, "You got something belongs to me."

"In the truck."

"Let's see it."

I threw a *here-goes-nothing* glance Shelby's way.

Then I started reaching inside the cab—

"Nice and slow," Coogler said, inching the flaming flare towards Harry.

With a glance at the shotgun in the footwell, I gripped the Gladstone medicine bag by the handle, trying not to betray the extra weight it contained as I lifted it off the seat, and then held it up for Coogler to see.

"Walk it over here," he said.

"Let Harry go first."

"Don't fuck with me, palooka! Walk it over here!" Coogler thrust the lighted road flare towards Harry.

Harry's eye bugged in terror and he turtle-tucked his head inside the gas-soaked tower of tires. "Reggie!" His voice echoed from inside the tires. "Do what he says, man!"

I dropped the bag at my feet, crossed my arms in defiance.

Coogler shook his head in exasperation. "You are one *stubborn* sonofabitch."

"Stubborn as a mule . . ." I said. "Or a jackass."

A smile cracked Coogler's lips. He drew the flare away from Harry and the tires. "How is the jackass?"

"He'll live," Shelby said.

"You know, I've never seen that before," Coogler said. "I mean, I've seen some fucked-up shit in my time, but I ain't never seen a man get dragged by a donkey-cock before."

I shot a sheepish glance at Shelby.

"What's he talking about?" she said.

"Nothing," I assured her. "He's crazy—"

"*Reggie Levine* . . ." Coogler crooned in a low, purring voice.

When someone says your name like that, like he knows your deepest darkest secrets, it's never good.

"Harry here's been telling us all about you, Reggie . . .

"But I knew I recognized your dumbass face from somewhere. When Billy and me was back in the pen—" Somehow I doubted he meant Penn State.

"We read all about that skunk ape thing." He cackled. "Tell me something: What kinda fucking moron mistakes a monkey for a monster?"

"You had to be there," I said. "While we're pointing fingers, reminding me what a dope I am—not that I'm arguing—you mind if I ask you a question?"

He gave a *let's-humor-this-asshole* smirk. "Shoot."

"Dude . . ." I chided him. "Who mules drugs in a donkey? *Really?*"

To Coogler's credit, he looked a little embarrassed. "Yeah, well. That's what happens when you delegate. I left it to Billy to arrange the mule. I figure, how hard could it be? Turns out, *real* fucking hard. Cuz Billy took what I said a little too literal. Next thing I know he's arranged for this veterinarian we met at a Brotherhood dogfight—one of your local boys, Edgar Dubrow—to have the jackass freighted from T.J. to Grabowski's. Billy says he's sorry; he tried, but he couldn't find a mule. I say to him, 'Billy, you dumb shit! I meant we use a beaner to mule the coke, someone no one's gonna miss when we cut him outta the deal!'" Coogler glared at Billy. "I didn't know better, I'd think Billy didn't want his operation, tried to screw the deal on purpose."

"Operation?" I said.

Coogler scissored his fingers, *snip-snip.*

Billy winced, shuddered, bowed his head.

"We're back in the straight world," Coogler said. "Ain't like the joint. Feels kinda faggoty I keep fucking Billy in the ass."

"So you fellas are jailhouse sweethearts?"

"Gotta problem with that?"

"Hell, no. It's the twenty-first century. You're both consenting adults."

Billy stifled a sob, and I wondered how consenting he really was.

"Soon as Billy has his operation," Coogler went on, "I'm gonna make an honest woman outta him."

"And they say romance is dead."

"After that, the two of us are gonna fly straight," Coogler said. "I always wanted to own my own coffee shop," he admitted with a wistful smile. Then the smile disappeared: "But now thanks to you, Billy's operation's gonna have to wait. The money we make on the coke's gonna pay to get Billy's face fixed." He looked at Billy and shuddered. "I mean: Would *you* fuck that?"

"If I'm honest," I said. "I've done worse."

Coogler laughed, despite himself.

"Alright . . ." he said. "Billy. Go get the bag."

Billy hesitated. "Whumee?"

"Bitch," Coogler hissed at him. "You're making me look bad—*Go!*"

Billy gave a heavy sigh and started hobbling towards me like a pistol-packing zombie. "Gunk goo fugga moob," he warned me, or gibberish to that effect.

I toed the medicine bag across the ground towards him.

Thinking: *Alright, Gizmo . . . Showtime.* So far the dog was playing his part to perfection; I hadn't heard a peep from inside the bag.

Billy crouched down awkwardly in front of the bag. He frowned. Couldn't figure out how to unclasp the bag with his claw, while keeping his gun trained on me with his able hand. He slapped his claw at the bag pathetically.

"I could hold the gun for you?" I offered.

"Shuggafuggugg!"

"Billy," Coogler called impatiently. "We good?"

Billy set the revolver on the ground by his feet. Using his claw to hold the bag still, he undid the clasp with his able hand, and then wrenched the bag open—

Gizmo sprang from the bag like a snaggletoothed jack-in-the-box, sinking his fangs into Billy's nose. Billy screeched, the dog dangling from his nose like a monstrous wriggling booger. It was all the distraction I needed. Snatching the shotgun from the truck, I scythed the stock across Billy's jaw, dropping him cold to the ground. Before Coogler torched the tires and roasted Harry alive, I fired the shotgun. The blast struck him in the chest, hurled him back against the Airstream, still clutching the flare in a death grip. Coogler crumpled to the ground, smearing blood down the trailer, a look of sheer disbelief on his face. I ditched the shotgun, and then I slung my arm around Shelby's dainty waist and pulled her roughly towards me. "Oh, Reggie . . ." she gasped, melting in my manly embrace. I mashed my lips against hers and her sensuous tongue pushed into my mouth and we kissed; long, deep and hungry.

That's how I'd pictured things panning out.

Especially the bit about Shelby's sensuous tongue.

Instead, what happened was Billy opened the bag and cried, "Ew! Whugga fugg!" He flailed with his claw and knocked the bag on its side and an avalanche of white powder spilled across the ground. The plastic wrapping around the bricks of cocaine was torn to shreds. Gizmo fell stiff-as-a-board from the bag. His snout was bloody. His eyes were big as hubcaps. His teeth were bared in an insane rictus. The dumb mutt had chewed through the plastic, devoured five bricks of uncut cocaine like it was powdered Scooby Snacks, and OD'd.

Shelby let out a cry of horror.

I stammered: "Doc, I had no idea—"

Coogler shouted at Billy, "What the fuck's going on?"

"Degg ragg!" Billy shouted back.

"What?"

"Dead! Rat!"

Then Coogler saw the spilled cocaine, and he roared: "Kill 'em! Kill 'em both!"

4.

Billy lurched for the revolver. With a sweep of my foot, I kicked the pile of coke in his eye like a bully at the beach kicking sand in the face of a wimp. Now blind in both eyes, his face frosted with white powder, Billy let out a cry and staggered back, choking and sputtering. I jacked an uppercut to his jaw. He collapsed in a jellied heap, cracking the back of his skull against the asphalt as he landed next to Gizmo's corpse. He was out cold—hell, maybe even dead—but I wasn't taking any chances; I kicked the revolver beyond his reach and it skittered away across the court.

"Billy!" Coogler cried.

He wheeled towards Harry to fling the flare—Shelby drew her pistol from the back of her jeans and fired, striking Coogler high in the shoulder and spinning him like a top. The flare dropped from Coogler's hand and landed dangerously close to the gasoline moat around the tower of tires. Coogler pulled his shotgun and fired back at Shelby. She took cover behind the open driver's-side door of the truck. Coogler's shot peppered the metal and shattered the glass. Shelby was knocked to the ground as if yanked by an invisible rope, falling from view behind the truck.

Then Coogler whipped the shotgun towards me. I leapt for cover behind the bank of cars to my right. Unable to vent his fury on me, Coogler kicked Harry's tower of tires over. The tower toppled to the ground with a heavy thud. Gasoline sprayed from the tires and splashed across the lighted flare. The moat of gas ignited with a woof of flames. But the tower, with Harry still trapped inside it, was already rolling away down the sloping court, and fast gathering speed. A shark fin of fire sizzled behind it, pursuing the tower as it rolled down the lot, spraying gasoline in its wake. Harry's head poked from the end of the tires. "Reeeeeeeeeeggieeeeeeeeee!"

Shelby lay on the ground next to her truck. She saw Harry and the tires hurtling towards her, pursued by the tongue of fire. Before she was flattened and flame-grilled, she rolled for cover beneath the truck. Harry screamed for help as he barreled past her, and continued to roll towards the open front gate. That's when Randy-Ray Gooch swung his Bronco through the gate. A logjam of plastic drums was bungee-roped in the bed of the truck. The sides of the barrels were stickered with hazardous waste and flammable warnings. The bucket seller was slumped beside Gooch with his head hung in shame and his hands cuffed behind him.

Randy-Ray cussed as he saw the ring of tires rocketing towards him like a giant rubber rolling pin, and the blazing tongue of fire hungering after it. He wrenched the steering wheel. The Bronco swerved violently, plowing nose-first into a bank of used-cars. Gooch and the bucket seller were thrown forwards in their seats, butting the wheel and the dash respectively. The airbags deployed milliseconds after impact, which, for Gooch, only added insult to injury.

The ring of tires rolled on through the front gate, across the street and finally thudded to a stop against a streetlamp. The impact had loosened the tires; as the fire snaked towards him, Harry managed to squirm free from the ring and scuttle away to safety. The tires burst into flames. Harry stripped off his gasoline-soaked clothes and capered naked in the firelight, gibbering like the caveman who invented fire, dancing a jig he was so happy to be alive.

5.

I raced to check on Shelby. She was lying on her back beneath the truck, a hand clamped to her shoulder, blood welling through her fingers. "You okay, Doc?"

Her eyes rolled towards me. "Hell, no. I've been

shot, you moron."

I grinned. "You've still got some sass, that's a good sign."

I helped her out from under the truck and then sat her up against it. Diamonds of broken glass rained from her hair. Her jersey was perforated where three of Coogler's shotgun pellets had ripped through her shoulder. But the truck door had taken the brunt of the blast. I stripped off my Hawaiian shirt, shamefully aware of the doughy gut drooping over my belt buckle, and my flabby pectoral muscles—hell, let's call 'em what they were: Man-tits. I wadded the shirt into a ball and Shelby clamped it over her wounded shoulder and staunched the bleeding.

"Where's Coogler?" she said.

"Took off towards the back of the lot."

"Well, go get that bastard."

I'd have preferred to wait for reinforcements, stayed where I was and comforted her. I sure as hell didn't fancy chasing after Coogler. I felt lucky just to be alive. Why tempt fate? "What about you?" Hoping she'd take the hint.

Shelby fetched her pistol, checked it, and set it in her lap. "I'll be fine."

"But I can't just leave you—"

"Go!"

Bitching under my breath, I left Shelby there and fetched Walt's shotgun from inside the truck. I racked a round in the chamber, sucked a deep breath, glanced back at Shelby to check if she'd changed her mind and wanted me to stay—nope.

Then I went after Coogler.

6.

Slumped against the truck, Shelby shut her eyes so she didn't have to look at Gizmo's pathetic, stiff-legged corpse on the ground next to Billy, who was still out cold. I can only imagine how terrible she felt; by allowing me to carry out the dumbass plan that'd led to Gizmo's death, she'd broken the veterinarian's Hippocratic oath. Hearing the sound of tortured metal, and broken glass tinkling to the ground, her eyes snapped open and she glanced across the lot.

Gooch was staggering from the wreck of his Bronco.

But before she could call to the lawman for help, a shadow fell across her—

Startled, she looked up and saw Billy looming over her.

Billy's eye blazed hatefully from a mask of white powder; he looked like a Cyclopean geisha gal. The coke I'd kicked in his face must have counteracted the tiger tranquilizer, ironed out his kinks and re-invigorated him.

Billy kicked the pistol from Shelby's hands, and then stamped on her wounded shoulder.

Shelby screamed, blacking-out from the pain—

Snapping back to consciousness to find Billy dragging her into her own truck.

Billy keyed the engine, crunched the truck into gear and hit the gas. As the truck lurched towards the front gate, Shelby reached across the cab and twisted the steering wheel in Billy's hands. The truck veered sharply towards Gooch's Bronco. Gooch saw the collision coming and dragged the bucket seller from the cab with just seconds to spare. Shelby flung her door open and leapt from the truck, hitting the ground and rolling to safety.

Billy could only scream as the truck broadsided Gooch's Bronco, crushing the plastic drums in the bed. The ruptured drums spewed their contents across the truck windshield in a flood of toxic slurry. The Plexiglas dissolved like sugar glass. There was a deafening hissing sound, as if all the snakes in creation had been loosed upon the dealership. The detergent poured inside the truck, filling the cab and enveloping Billy like The Blob devouring a victim. Shelby watched in horror as a hand slapped helplessly against the driver's-side window. The skin sloughed away from the palm to reveal the bleached bones beneath. The door clattered open. A waterfall of detergent cascaded steaming to the ground. Billy staggered from the truck. The flesh was melting from his face like candle wax. He guttered and gurgled, took a few shambling steps, before flopping facedown in the seething pool of detergent. Billy's corpse shuddered as it was boiled down to a vaguely man-shaped stain on the asphalt forecourt.

Randy-Ray grasped his swollen testicles in a quasi-religious gesture. He said to the bucket seller, "What the hell do you *put* in that shit?"

The bucket seller gaped at the carnage. "Trade secrets."

Then he frowned at the trail of fire.

The chemical spillage frothed angrily in the heat of the flames.

"But I'll tell you one thing," he said, "it sure don't mix with fire."

"Oh, that's just great," Randy-Ray said. "Alright, get moving, fuckstick." He shoved the bucket seller towards the front gate, with a kick in the ass to hurry him along. "Wait out front. You even think about running, I'll make you gargle that shit."

Randy-Ray went and helped Shelby to her feet.

"The hell's going on here, Doc?"

Too dazed to speak, she could only shake her head.

"Walt said it was an emergency," Gooch said. "Something about Reggie and a donkey-cock . . ."

He gazed across the sea of cars towards the back of the dealership.

"Where *is* Reggie, anyway?"

7.

I was threading through the gridlock of used-cars, crouching low for cover to avoid Coogler's shots, returning his fire with blasts from Walt's shotgun, and slowly gaining ground on him.

Reaching the last line of cars between Coogler and me, I ducked for cover behind a rusted Plymouth, and caught my breath. Coogler's shotgun roared and the side windows exploded above my head and showered me with glass.

I didn't know how Coogler was fixed for ammo, but I was down to my last round. I needed to make it count.

But there it went, whizzing harmlessly over Coogler's head, wasted. I tossed the empty shotgun away. Coogler was hunkered down behind the Toronado. Before either of us could make a move, we were distracted by Randy-Ray's arrival, and Billy fleeing in Shelby's truck. When Coogler saw the horrific collision, and Billy melt into a puddle like the Wicked Prison Bitch of the West, he screamed in grief and rage.

"You're a fucking dead man, Levine! You hear me! Dead!"

But revenge could wait. The law had arrived, and now Coogler was outnumbered. He leapt in the Toronado, keyed the ignition, hit the gas, the engine roared like the devil in hell, and the car sped away in a twister of tire smoke. The Toronado was racing parallel to the line of cars I was huddled behind; in seconds it would pass me.

I could have let him go.

In hindsight, I should have.

Instead I vaulted up onto the trunk of the Plymouth, scrambled across the roof and prepared to fling myself onto the speeding Toronado as Coogler tore past. I'd seen TJ Hooker do it dozens of times in the old TV cop show; anything Shatner could do, so could I. Then I stepped on the sunroof, the glass shattered beneath my bulk, and my leg plunged hip-deep inside the Plymouth.

I watched helplessly as the Toronado rocketed past me and burst through the chain link fence at the back of the lot. Coogler was gone into the night.

Well, the hell with it. Coogler was the law's

problem now. I'd done what I could—played hero—and looked where it'd got me: Snagged in the sunroof of a fucking Plymouth. I laughed in exasperation. Could things get any worse?

Dumb question.

As I attempted to extract my leg from the sunroof, two things happened.

The first was I realized I was stuck fast; the jagged glass teeth of the shattered sunroof were biting into my thigh like pit bull jaws.

The second was an H-bomb exploded at the front of the lot.

At least, that was my first thought when the detergent detonated.

There was a blinding white flash of light, and then a brilliant column of fire billowed up into the night, as if a portal had opened to another dimension.

The boom of the blast shattered windshields and windows. Car alarms started blaring an off-key symphony of *La Cucaracha*. The shockwave stormed through the lot. I raised my hands to shield my eyes, but the heat blast scorched my hair and even my eyelashes. Flaming sales stickers, replete with Harry's mugging caricature, twisted in the sky like party streamers. A hailstorm of burning beaters rained down from the heavens, crushing vehicles the blast had not already obliterated. These vehicles exploded in turn, until the lines of cars began exploding like chains of firecrackers. A monstrous tsunami of fire rushed towards me like a surging sea of napalm.

Stuck in the sunroof, I looked around helplessly as the great wall of fire roared towards me, devouring everything in its path, setting off explosions that tossed cars through the air like kids' toys.

I cast my eyes plaintively to the heavens . . . And saw the web of bunting roped above the lot, the plastic pennants melting like grilled cheese. I reached for the rope above me, straining my arm to full extension. My fingertips brushed the rope, but I couldn't get a grip to pull it down. In desperation, I lunged upwards, crying out as the jagged glass dug deeper into my thigh. I grabbed the rope and started hauling on it, trying to pull myself from the sunroof. The inflatable Harry on the roof of the trailer, buffeted by the explosions, seemed to be nodding his encouragement. I pulled at the rope with all my might, ignoring the stabbing pain in my leg, roaring and cursing as the flames rushed towards me. Only five cars away. Four, three . . . With the last of my strength, I yanked at the rope, and suddenly the inflatable Harry's legs did an Elvis-shimmy, like a marionette dancing for a drunken puppeteer. The mooring ropes began unraveling, snapping and whipping through the air—

And then the balloon man tore away from the trailer roof, soaring up into the night sky at terrifying speed, propelled by the blast of the explosions and the baking heat of the fire. Ropes trailed beneath the balloon man like jellyfish tendrils . . . including, I suddenly realized, the very rope I was holding onto.

I was yanked from the sunroof like a mouse snatched up by a swooping hawk. Broken glass lacerated my thigh, ripping the leg of my jeans into a single Daisy Duke cutoff. And then I soared up into the sky, dangling by the length of rope beneath the hot-air-Harry. Below me, the burning car dealership was a map of hell. The wall of fire reached the Plymouth from which I'd just escaped, and now it too exploded into a fireball. I tucked my legs to prevent my feet being roasted by the grasping flames. The explosion buffeted the balloon man and me higher into the sky, and we floated up, up and away from the scorching heat and flames . . . up into the cool night air.

8.

I breezed above the street at the front of the lot, clinging to the rope beneath the hot-air Harry. Gazing down, the scene unfolded beneath me like something from a dream.

Gooch and the handcuffed bucket seller were watching the dealership burn like spectators at a fireworks show, ooh-ing and aah-ing at the exploding cars.

Harry sobbed as his whole world went up in flames. He was still naked, his hands cupped over his privates. When the Airstream trailer went up, launched into the sky like a Cape Canaveral rocket, Harry's hands fell away from his genitals and he sank to his knees; if it wasn't for his look of abject despair, he could've been a pyromaniac exposing himself to the inferno.

Shelby was sitting on the curb, nursing her wounded shoulder, the Hawaiian shirt I'd given her to staunch the wound soaked through with blood. Her eyes glistened with tears. Was she weeping from the pain of her wounded shoulder? Did she just have smoke in her peepers? Or was she grieving me, believing I had perished in the fire? I was hoping on the latter.

She glanced up, saw me floating above them, and did a double take.

"Levine?"

I can only imagine how I looked: Dangling by a rope from a giant floating balloon man, shirtless, wearing half a pair of jeans, with gravity making a mockery of my naked gut and man-tits.

Without the heat of the flames to keep the balloon aloft, my weight was starting to tell, and the hot-air Harry descended, gently lowering me to the sidewalk. I released the rope and stepped away, as casually as a commuter disembarking public transport. Then I collapsed on my ass on the curb next to Shelby.

I smiled at her stupidly. "How're you holding up, Doc?"

Shelby watched as the hot-air Harry drifted back up into the night sky. She started to say something, but seemed lost for words. Composing herself, she tried again. "I, uh—I think I'll be okay. You?"

"Was hoping you could tell me."

With a hiss of pain, I extended my bleeding leg.

She leaned forward and examined it, her hands oh, so gentle.

"You're lucky."

I wheezed laughter. "This is what that feels like, huh?"

"If those cuts were any deeper, you'd have severed your femoral artery; you'd be dead already."

"But I'm not gonna lose the leg?"

She shook her head.

"Good," I said. "Then maybe I can take you dancing sometime?"

Sometimes all it takes to grow a pair is a near-death experience.

Shelby winced in discomfort. "Reggie—"

"Hey!" I grinned. "You said my name."

"I like women," she said.

"Then we got that in common." I tipped her a wink. Then I said, "Oh . . ."

Then I fell silent.

She put her good arm around my shoulder.

I choked down the lump in my throat.

"I'm sure there's someone else out there for you, Reggie."

I was already sick of her saying my name. "You really think so, Doc?"

If she answered, I didn't hear her; not over the sound of the last of Harry's cars exploding, and the banshee-wail of the approaching EMS sirens.

SEVEN

THE SMELL OF HARRY'S PRE-OWNED AMERICAN AUTO IN THE MORNING

1.

It was déjà vu all over again. I was back in the same hospital, same room, same bed, same Mrs. Antwone poisoning me with her cooking, as after the Backseat Strangler thing. About the only difference was the level of pain I was suffering.

The patron saint of bouncers, Dalton, once said: "Pain don't hurt." Far be it from me to disagree, but Dalton was wrong: Pain hurts like a motherfucker.

It looked like a shark had savaged my leg; my thigh was a Frankenstein's Monster of mangled meat, stitched and stapled and swathed in bandages.

My shoulder throbbed like the throwing arm of a big league pitcher. I'd been lucky my arm wasn't wrenched from the socket when the balloon man yanked me from the sunroof. Hell, I'd been lucky not to lose my other arm when I was dragged behind Enrique. My body was hashtagged with cuts, covered in grazes, and what wasn't cut or grazed had been bruised or baked in the fire, leaving me bronzed as a seedy Vegas lounge singer. My hair was singed to a stubbly crewcut. My ears were whining with tinnitus. I had a concussion . . .

And worst of all, Shelby Boon had broken my heart.

On my nightstand was an oversize GET WELL SOON card with a picture of a sad-looking bear with his paw in a sling. The gals at The Henhouse, and a bunch of the regulars, had chipped in to buy the card, and then signed it during an epic bender, if the handwriting inside was anything to go by.

Even Walt had signed the card:

See you back at work, Champ.

He'd also attached a receipt for the shotgun I'd lost in the fire.

2.

Shelby was discharged from hospital before me, and came to say goodbye on checking-out day. Her arm was in a sling, like the bear on my card. Her wounds had proved to be superficial. The shotgun pellets had passed through her shoulder without causing major damage. What they call in the movies, "Just a scratch." With Shelby that day was a strapping young gal—tall, dark and handsome—with close-cropped hair and a handshake like a lumberjack.

"Reggie," Shelby introduced us. "This is my friend, Kimber."

I tried not to wince as Kimber pumped my hand.

"Mr. Levine," she said, "I wanted to thank you for making sure Shelby made it home alive."

I didn't know how big a part I'd played in that, but I've never been above taking undue credit. "All part of the service."

Kimber looked lovingly at Shelby.

"Anything happened to my woman," she said, "I'd plain lose my mind."

The way they were gazing into each other's eyes, I wondered should I yank the IV-drip from my arm and give them the room; it was getting mighty toasty in there. Then Kimber dragged Shelby into her arms and kissed her just the way I'd imagined I'd be kissing her, sensuous tongue and all. My throat went dry. I swallowed hard. It felt like they were kissing so long the nurses changed shift. To Shelby's credit, she seemed uncomfortable with me being there and withdrew from the embrace. She wiped Kimber's lipstick from her mouth and readjusted her sling, which had got a little rumpled. "Reggie doesn't want to see this."

Well, I didn't and I did, you know.

Shelby leaned over my bed and brushed my hair

from my forehead like she was taking my temperature. After seeing what I'd seen, it was probably a little high.

She said, "Get better, tough guy."

Then she pecked me on the cheek like a sister kissing her kid brother.

"Feeling better already," I lied.

Shelby straightened up and Kimber took her hand, and then they left the room together, and I was left alone. Racked with a symphony of pain, both inside and out, I thought again about what that damn fool Dalton said, "Pain don't hurt."

Maybe one day, given time, and enough booze, I'd be able to convince myself that the only reason things hadn't worked out between Shelby and me, was because all along she'd preferred girls.

3.

By the time Harry got around to visiting me, and I hadn't been holding my breath, he'd been fitted with a new glass eye. He was still getting used to it. When the eye wasn't staring at his nose, it'd swivel about the socket like the peeper of a possessed ventriloquist's dummy, or glance suddenly over my shoulder as if someone was looming behind me, making me jumpy. He'd also shaved his mustache, maybe as some kind of penance; like Tom Selleck, Harry looked weird without facial hair, his upper lip oddly exposed and vulnerable.

Harry scraped a chair next to my bed, and placed

the urn he was carrying on his lap. "Gizmo," he said, in a reverent voice. I averted my eyes, guilty. "At least, I hope there's some of him in here. I shoveled up what I could. It's hard to tell for sure. The lot is some kinda mess." He shook his head solemnly, for Gizmo or his car dealership, I couldn't say.

"You're insured, right?"

He gave a bitter bark of laughter.

"Sure. The insurance should just about cover the cost of the divorce lawyer."

Turns out, Mrs. Muffet's kennel club conference in London, England had in fact been a ruse. Suspecting her husband of infidelity, Mrs. Muffet had hired a gumshoe to monitor his movements while she was away. The photos of Harry and his secretary Miss Clemens 'working late' proved more than sufficient grounds for divorce in Mrs. Muffet's favor.

"She's cleaning me out," Harry said.

I vaguely recalled him telling me that everything he owned was signed in his wife's name. For business reasons, he'd said.

When I failed to produce a violin from under my pillow, and start playing him a sad song, Harry said, "I'm hoping, I give her what's left of Gizmo—" He shook the urn and rattled the cremains: "—maybe she'll take me back."

I thought he shouldn't count on it. "And if she doesn't?"

He gave a self-pitying shake of his head that swiveled his glass eye towards his ear. "Damned if I know. Start over, I guess."

"Harry . . ." I broke it to him gently. "Have you

ever considered, everything that's happened, it's been a sign from the Man Upstairs to change your ways?"

Not bad advice, now that I thought about it.

"Pretty drastic sign, dontcha think?"

"Well, maybe He's been sending you a bunch of smaller signs, only you've had your head stuck so far up your ass you haven't noticed?"

Harry stroked his upper lip where his mustache had been. I was starting to suspect he hadn't shaved it himself, after all, that the doctors had shaved it for him. He appeared to be giving what I'd said serious thought, but I knew it'd been in one ear, out the other, and it wouldn't be long before he was neck-deep in some other shit. The difference was, when it happened, I wouldn't be there to bail him out. From herein, Harry Muffet was on his own. My heroing days were over.

Harry said: "Listen, Reggie. For what it's worth, I'm sorry I got you mixed up in this. Who knew, am I right? Thanks for saving my life, man." He chuckled. "I guess this makes us even, huh?" He saw my expression and quickly said, "Of course, I can see how you might view things a little different. So with that in mind—as just a small token of my appreciation . . ."

He fished in his pocket and produced a set of keys.

"I thought you lost everything in the fire?"

"I did," he said. "Repo'd this baby last night."

I laughed, despite myself. "You're some piece of work, Harry."

He tossed me the keys and nodded at the window. "She's right outside."

I dragged myself from bed, hobbled to the window and peered down into the parking lot. All I saw was an '82 Chevy Wideside. Painted on the hood was a bloody-beaked pterodactyl, its membranous wings extended as it screeched from the fiery pits of hell; the kind of paintjob I would've gladly splurged six-months wages on. Attached above the front bumper was a gleaming chrome winch; dangling from the rear a pair of ornamental brass testicles.

I strained to see if there was a piece-of-shit Pinto tucked behind the Wideside.

"Where is it?"

"You're looking at it," Harry said.

"Are you shitting me?"

"Just like Lee Majors drove in *The Fall Guy!*" Harry said, beaming. "Now the divorce lawyers don't know about this, so mum's the word." He tapped his nose slyly and his glass eye jittered in the socket. "We cool?"

I hated myself for being so susceptible to bribery.

"Harry—I don't know what to say."

"How about sorry for killing my wife's dog?"

I winced. "Jesus, Harry—I *am* sorry about that!"

He cracked a smile. "Ah, don't be," he said. "I always hated that ugly fucking mutt."

He stood up to leave, juggling the urn from hand to hand before tucking it under his arm. "See you 'round, Reggie."

I gave a weary laugh as he walked out the door. *Christ, I hoped not.*

4.

When my medication was reduced, and I was back to being my borderline coherent self, Randy-Ray Gooch came to take my statement. He'd spared me a lot of the legal red tape that ensues when a bungled drug deal cum kidnap for ransom results in an explosion big enough to level a used-car dealership. I'd still have my day in court—I'd gotten away with kayoing a jackass, but somehow PETA had learned about my involvement in the cocaine overdose of a Chinese crested terrier—but for now, Gooch said I'd earned a break.

He pulled up a chair and straddled it backwards.

Pretty nimble for a guy in his condition, I thought, but didn't say anything.

"Any word on Coogler?" I asked.

"Still at large," Gooch said, resisting the urge to spit on the hospital room floor in righteous anger. "We found his car out at Beetner's Leap, but no one's buying he took the plunge. Hell, not even Beetner hisself leapt from that bluff."

Beetner's Leap was a notorious suicide spot, named after a scam artist who'd attempted to outwit his creditors by faking his death. It hadn't worked. The goons had eventually collared Beetner and hurled him from the very same bluff. Since then, the name had stuck, much like Beetner when he hit the ground.

Gooch seemed certain Coogler was long gone, most likely being sheltered by the neo-Nazi underground railroad. "All this heat on him, the man would have to be crazy coming after you now," Gooch said, with the confidence of a man whose own ass wasn't on the line.

"He *is* crazy," I reminded him.

"There is that," Gooch said. "Yeah, probably best you keep your eyes open till we drop the net on him. Fact is, the more I hear about this Mitchell Coogler sonofabitch, the more it turns the hairs on my balls white."

I caught the twinkle in his eye.

"The hair on your—" I said, "It grew back?"

"Every strand." Gooch grinned. "Seems just catching the bucket seller was enough. I always reckoned it was psychological."

"Good for you, Randy-Ray."

He nodded proudly. "Anyways . . ." He produced a bulging file folder.

Coogler's file contained a flipbook of mugshots.

It was startling to see the man's transformation from a juvenile, into the Mitchell Coogler I knew and loathed—piling on the muscle over the years, desecrating his flesh with jailhouse ink, experimenting with various styles of facial hair: Full-beard, Handlebars, Fu Manchu, Soul Patch, Hitler, of course, until finally, Circus Strongman. Only those stone-cold killer's eyes remained the same.

"Mitchell Coogler . . . He's got a rap sheet as long as that jackass' pecker. Made his bones as an enforcer for the Aryan Brotherhood. He's been in and out of the joint ever since he was old enough to burn a cross. Always bullshit charges. Nothing that could ever put him down in the hole for life. The way Coogler's slipped through the cracks in the System, it's like he's some kinda Teflon Nazi."

Gooch turned to the next file.

"Coogler's cellmate, William aka Billy aka 'Kermit the Frog' Barnes . . ."

Billy's mugshot showed the punk squinting through a mask of frog-green paint.

"He's what you might call a natural born fuckup."

"Sounds familiar," I said. "Why's he green like this?"

"I'll get to that."

The last file, and the most recent mugshot, showed Edgar Dubrow. He was sneering into the camera, unrepentant as a Nuremberg Nazi. "You already know this shitbird," Gooch said. "We picked up Dubrow, put his feet to the fire till he squealed. Between what Dubrow told us, and the statement you made, here's what we know . . ."

5.

Billy Barnes must have wondered how his life might've panned out, he hadn't robbed that savings and loan. It'd seemed like a sweet deal at the time. A quick dollar stickup to buy his sweetheart Charlene that engagement ring she had her heart set on, and to give them a start in life. He'd planned it all carefully, and to Billy's credit the robbery itself went off without a hitch. It was the getaway was the problem. He was fleeing the bank with the cash in a sack when the dye-pack exploded, coating the kid in Kermit-green paint that blinded and burned, left him balled on the sidewalk in hot agony, easy for the cops to scrape up. The arresting officer said to his partner: "Jeez, you think this is the guy?" They still laughed about it when they told the story.

Six-months into Billy's prison bit, the dye had hardly faded. It had proved next to impossible for the first time felon to project a *don't-fuck-with-me* aura when he looked like a Muppet. With his boyish looks, and a funny arrest story to share on the yard, Billy Barnes became a popular young man among many of the more hardened convicts. It sure as hell wasn't easy being green.

Fortunately his new cellmate, Mitchell Coogler, had been there to take Billy under his wing—and into his bunk, the latter being a small price to pay for Coogler's protection from the other jailhouse rapists. At least, that's the positive spin Billy tried to put on things, the first night he wadded his ruptured asshole with toilet paper.

Of course, he had tried to explain to Coogler that he was not homosexual. That he was, in fact, engaged to be married. (Billy was still holding out hope that he could patch things up with Charlene; she'd sent him a Dear John note following his arrest.) Coogler had listened to Billy politely, apologized for the misunderstanding, and then proceeded to beat the punk to an inch of his life.

Billy regained consciousness with scrambled brains, missing teeth, a burning butt, and the overwhelming urge to do anything Coogler told him if it saved him from future beatings.

For three long years, Billy bit his pillow and

counted down the days till the end of his sentence. Coogler was released six months before Billy. This wasn't the blessing Billy had at first assumed. Coogler had simply passed him on to his Brotherhood brothers for 'safekeeping.' Presumably, he'd also told them: "And help yourself to all the rump you can pump," because they sure as hell had.

The day of Billy's release, determined never to return to jail, punished and rehabilitated in the most painful way possible, he'd hobbled from the big house . . .

Only to find Coogler's black Toronado waiting for him in the parking lot.

"Get in," Coogler said, leering at Billy like a Tex Avery wolf. "It's been six months. We gotta lotta catching up to do."

Billy didn't understand.

"I—I thought what happened was a jailhouse thing?"

Coogler nodded, as if he'd thought the same. "Tried it with a woman when I got out," he said. "Didn't take. Truth is, I—I love you, Billy-boy . . . Now get in."

"But—"

"Bitch, don't make me tell you twice."

Billy glanced back plaintively at the watchtower guard.

The guy smirked and turned his back on Billy.

Billy trudged to the car like a condemned man going to the gallows.

After getting reacquainted at a hot-sheet motel, the lovebirds celebrated Billy's release with a cultural evening at a neo-Nazi dogfight. It was there they met disgraced former vet, Edgar Dubrow, who was officiating as a pit-side medic. Later, when Coogler hatched his drug-smuggling scheme to pay for Billy's sex-change operation, Billy had recruited Dubrow to mule the drugs inside Enrique under the guise of an animal rescue. Dubrow arranged for Enrique to be shipped from down Mexico way to Grabowski's Gas & Zoo. Coogler and Billy waited a week to assess if the cops were wise to their plan. When the coast was clear they came to collect Enrique. Which, unfortunately for Muffet and me, happened to be the very same day we were retrieving Gizmo from Grabowski . . .

6.

"And the rest is history," Gooch said.

I shook my head and said, "Could've happened to anyone."

Gooch laughed and started gathering the mugshots back inside the file folder.

"Sheriff Jaynes hasn't come seen me yet," I said.

"Careful what you wish for."

"He still mad about the Strangler thing?"

"Ho, boy. Real fucking mad," Gooch said. "And this 'Showdown at Harry's Pre-Owned American Auto' business hasn't helped cool him off."

Showdown at Harry's Pre-Owned American Auto

That's the headline the *Bigelow Bugle* gave what'd happened.

Not quite the *Gunfight at the O.K. Corral.*
The photo that accompanied the front-page article was far from flattering. The shutterbug must've bribed an orderly, snuck into my hospital room while I was hopped-up on painkillers, and snapped me with my eyes in orbit, tongue lolling from my catching-flies mouth, and a puddle of drool on the chest of my hospital johnny. For all the world, I looked like one of Eliza Tuttle's mongoloids, sated from the services of a comfort nurse. I just knew that Walt would be adding the picture to my Wall of Shame at The Henhouse, if he hadn't already done so.

Gooch said, "Maybe if you'd actually *caught* Coogler, 'stead of letting him get away . . . ?" He shrugged.

"Yeah, right," I grumbled, "my bad."

Gooch stood up to leave.

"Listen. When you're back on your feet, come see me at the stationhouse. We'll take about getting you deputized. If you insist on getting yourself into this shit then it's best you're wearing a badge, if only to keep the Sheriff off your back."

I thanked Gooch, and told him I'd consider his offer, but the truth was all I could think about was my regular spot at The Henhouse. Sitting at my end of the slab with an ice-cold Coors and a copy of *Ring* magazine, and nothing more stressful to deal with than an ID to check, or a drunk to turf out . . .

And as soon as I was discharged from the hospital, that's where I went.

Back to what I knew, and maybe, like Walt once said, back where I belonged.

EIGHT

GET TO THE CHOPPER!

1.

Just another any old afternoon at The Henhouse. Small crowd of regulars; Marlene working the stage to lusty howls from the men; Lou parked at his spot at the end of the runway. Marlene seemed a little ticked she didn't have Lou's undivided attention, not to mention the bushel of bucks in her G-string that went with it. But Lou was otherwise occupied. Like a proud new father, he was showing anyone he could the photos of Enrique on his camera phone; photos of the jackass grazing harmlessly in Lou's backyard, I hoped, and not performing again.

I don't know quite how Lou managed it, which palms he greased, but somehow he'd been permitted to adopt Enrique; Shelby had worked tirelessly to ensure that the rest of Grabowski's menagerie found good homes, or were euthanized as humanely as possible. The Lou and Enrique situation reminded me of that Stephen King movie with Jimmy Caan and Kathy Bates. Any day now I expected to hear that Hank Sanderson had loaned Lou his video camera, and that *The Famous Mr. Head* was launching a comeback.

I was sitting at my spot at the end of the slab, with a bottle of Coors and *The Ring* magazine, living the dream I'd had in the hospital. My wounded leg was elevated on the barstool beside me. It was healing nicely, if not prettily. Soon the stitches would come out, and the sawbones would decide if another round of skin grafts was in order. I hoped not. My ass hairs quite clearly didn't match my leg hairs, and any more skin grafts and my knee would start farting.

I'd been back at work almost a month now. Light duties. Business as usual, you could say. Walt sure as hell did.

Walt seemed happy to have me back. He never said as much, of course. That wasn't Walt's style. But every so often, I'd catch him looking at me with misty eyes, and then he'd gaze away across the barroom, like Alexander the Great in *Die Hard*, weeping 'cause he had no more worlds left to conquer. Except for the recipe for his Skunk Ape cocktail. Walt was still working on that.

The men's room was still out of order following my tussle with Otis, which felt like it'd happened another lifetime ago. Walt had casually suggested I might sell my new truck—she was parked out front—to pay for the damages. I laughed in his face and told him like hell.

The *Smokey and the Bandit* pinball machine had not been replaced, or even moved from the corner where it had collapsed, lying there shrouded in tarp. I figured Walt was waiting for my leg to fully heal, then he'd have me lug it to the junkyard to sell for scrap. I'd been robbed of the chance to earn back my high score. But with the machine out of action, I was actually saving a little money. All those quarters sure added up. And the extra money came in handy because Sue and me had been courting since I left the hospital.

Who's Sue? you ask.

Well, I'll tell you anyway.

Sue was the one ray of sunshine in the otherwise gloomy forecast of my life.

You may recall that my landlady, Mrs. Gowran, who ran the thrift store below my flophouse, had been threatening to match-make me with her niece.

While I was laid up in hospital, I'd had no choice but to indulge her.

Her timing was impeccable; I was taking a leak into my pisspot when Mrs. Gowran bustled into the room with a cheery "Yoo-hoo, Reggie!"

I said, "Jeez, Mrs. G, could I get two shakes here?" I've never been one of those clever dicks who can stop pissing once he's started; that's like magic to me.

Mrs. Gowran had brought me a fresh change of clothes from home, and some men's adventure novels—literature, she called it—to help pass the time.

She'd also brought her niece with her.

My fears that Sue would resemble her brother were quite unfounded; I could only assume one of them was adopted. She was pocketsize-petite, with a heart-shaped face, a cute button nose, a bob of blond hair, and bush-baby-big blue eyes.

She worked as a bookkeeper, and since her divorce, had volunteered at a shelter for victims of domestic violence. Maybe that's why Mrs. Gowran thought we'd get along? Sue and me, we're both protectors. 'Course, helping battered wives was a sight more noble that protecting strippers from stage invaders, or randy jackasses. But still . . . Same ballpark.

"Reggie," Mrs. Gowran said, "I'd like you to meet—" Then she saw I had my hands beneath the sheets, and that I was gripping what appeared to be an Enrique-sized phallus. (I wish.) "Oh!" she cried, getting the wrong end of the stick completely. She started herding the girl from the room. "Out, child, out!"

Squeezing out the drips, I said, "Wait! It's not what it looks like."

Of course, what it actually *was* wasn't much better. I snatched the sloshing pisspot from under the covers, and raised it aloft like I was making a toast.

To cover my blushes, all I could think to say was, "Good to meetcha."

Despite this inauspicious start, Sue agreed to see me again.

Our first date, we went to the pictures in Ayresville, where *Damn Dirty Apes* was playing at a midnight movie house. The movie was Sue's choice. I'm not *that* big a hotdog. But I guessed a little of that ole Nicolas Cage magic couldn't hurt. After the show, Sue asked me, "Did it really happen like that?"

"Pretty much," I admitted. "Apart from the scene

with the bear cub."

"Did you meet Nicolas Cage?"

"I wish. But he's a good guy. Even sent me a watch as a thank you."

Of course, she asked to see the watch.

I told her I'd lost it during that nasty business at Grabowski's, which was half-true. Sue didn't have to know the full story. That was between Enrique and me. What happened at Grabowski's Gas & Zoo, would stay at Grabowski's Gas & Zoo.

Since then, Sue and me had seen each other a bunch more times. It was still early days, but fair to say I was smitten. I'd started shaving semi-regular, quit drinking before noon most days; I even bought myself a whole new snazzy wardrobe from the Wal-Mart. Walt had voiced his concerns at the new and improved me, and accused me of putting on airs. I didn't care. This ole Rocky might've finally found his Adrian. Life was about as good as I'd known it. I even stopped checking over my shoulder for the fugitive Mitchell Coogler.

That, I would soon discover, was a mistake.

2.

Walt slammed a cocktail glass down in front of me, using my new copy of *Ring* magazine as a coaster. "Think I finally nailed the recipe," he said. I glanced along the slab at the barfly lab rats who'd been rendered unconscious by Walt's previous attempts. I took a cautious sip of the cocktail. "Not bad, huh?"

"Nope," I said, gagging. "Plain 'bad' ain't the word for it."

Walt flapped a bar towel at me. "What the hell do you know? Sue's ruined your palate with that fancy French wine she makes you drink." Walt was suspicious of wine-drinkers, and France in general. As far as Walt was concerned, even Thunderbird was 'fancy' and 'French.' Not that Sue and me caught the Night Train on our dates. Sue's a little classier than that.

Before I could retort—

The barroom started shaking. Bottles rattled on the back-bar shelves. One by one, the barflies awoke from their Skunk Ape-induced comas, their heads snapping up like startled lemurs. Marlene hugged her dance-pole like a sailor clutching the mast in a tempest. The Hank Williams record on the jukebox started skipping; it sounded like Hank was rapping. One of my framed news cuttings fell from the wall, the glass frame shattering on the floor.

My first thought: I was experiencing the aftereffects of Walt's Skunk Ape cocktail.

My second thought: *Coogler.*

"What is it?" Walt shouted above the noise, "Damn earthquake?"

"Not in Bigelow," I shouted back, with an ominous feeling.

Then the chopper swooped down from the sky. It hovered above The Henhouse like a giant black wasp, before slowly descending, skids raking the parking lot asphalt as it touched down. The blast from the rotor blades rattled my new truck and the other parked vehicles. The rear passenger door slid open . . . And then a familiar, shapely, blonde-haired, blue-eyed vision leapt out.

"Mr. Walt! Mr. Levine!" Eliza squealed, in her June Carter-on-crank voice.

We hadn't seen Eliza Tuttle since the skunk ape thing, after which she'd upped stakes for Hollywood, and found fame as a B-movie starlet in the *Damn Dirty Apes* movie. She waved at us, and we winced, seeing how close she'd come to sticking her hand into the roaring rotor.

Eliza came rushing inside and threw herself on me. My bum leg buckled under her weight, but I was so glad to see her, I hardly even noticed the pain.

Then it was Walt's turn. He gave her a paternal pat on the fanny, and then somewhat less paternally—unless you're Josef Fritzl—left his hand there.

Before we'd recovered from the shock of seeing Eliza, a second passenger climbed from the back of the chopper.

"Holy shit!" Walt gasped, when he saw who it was.

The face was vaguely equine: A prize stallion. The nose: Roman. The eyes: Heavenly blue. The Hollywood smile required a welder's mask to admire. He was wearing his *Damn Dirty Apes* hairpiece: A long gnarly mullet that made his *Con Air*-'do look like a buzzcut. Maybe he expected me to be wearing my hair the same way, and the hairpiece was to put me at ease? Or maybe he'd just grown fond of the style? As he crossed the parking lot and entered the Henhouse, the regulars fell into an awed silence. He extended his hand towards me, and I reached to shake it, reminded of the painting on the Sistine

Chapel ceiling. "Reggie Levine . . ." His voice was the velvety drugged-out drawl we all know and love.

"Mr. Cage," I breathed, star-struck as I shook The Man's hand.

"I've been trying to reach you," he told me. "You're tougher to get on the phone than my agent."

"That was really you calling?" I said, mortified. "I—I figured it was one of these jokers jerking my chain. Hell, Mr. Cage. If I'd known it was really you, I never would have called you none of that stuff. I actually *like* the bee movie."

Walt cleared his throat loudly.

"Mr. Cage," I said, "I'd like you to meet—"

Walt thrust his hand at Cage. "Walton Wiley: Proprietor."

"Nice place," Cage said, frowning at the blood-stained pool table. He glanced at the *Damn Dirty Apes* poster Walt had signed in his name. "I see we've met before?"

Walt chuckled sheepishly. "Wet your whistle, Mr. Cage?"

Beaming with pride, Walt mixed a fresh Skunk Ape cocktail and passed it across the bar. Cage picked up the cocktail, raised the glass to his lips, caught a whiff of the foul concoction, put the glass back down and said, "A cold beer will be fine."

Cage turned towards me. "Reggie, is there somewhere we can talk?"

I motioned to an unoccupied booth. "Let's take a pew . . . Walt, bring us a pitcher of Coors, would you?"

As I led the way, Cage said, "You're not wearing the watch?"

"That's quite a story. I'll tell you all about it."
Cage and me slid into the booth next to the
shrouded corpse of the pinball machine. Walt brought
us over the pitcher of beer, giving me the stink-eye for
making him wait on me. I gave him a grin. "Thank
you, *garcon*."
Walt saw the crowd watching us. "Mind your
business," he told them. "Carry on with your carryin'
on. You're all acting like you never seen a Hollywood
superstar in The Henhouse before."
Cage cocked an eyebrow at that. I told him, "Steve
Guttenberg was doing dinner theater in Ayresville.
He got lost on the way, come inside for directions."
"And then stayed for a week," Walt cut in. "That
damn Gutty's an animal."
"That'll be all, Walt. Thank you." I dismissed him
with a regal roll of my wrist.
Walt gritted his teeth and glared at me as he returned to his post behind the slab. But Eliza cheered
him up; asked if she could dance, for old times' sake.
Walt eagerly gave her a quarter from the register,
which should tell you how keen he was to see her
dance again. Eliza skipped across the room to the
jukebox and chose a record. Bad Company's *Feel Like
Makin Love* started booming through the speakers.
Marlene, who in Eliza's absence had become the
Henhouse's dancing queen, surrendered the stage
with strained good grace. She went and sat with Lou,
feigning interest in his photos of Enrique, she'd seen
'em all before.
As we watched Eliza shimmy out of her clothes,
I asked Cage how she was getting along out in

Hollywood; I hated to think she was being exploited by those seedy showbiz types. Cage assured me she was doing fine. I was happy for Eliza. Unlike me, she'd managed to turn her fifteen minutes of fame into a career. She'd sure come a long way since her days as a comfort nurse, attending to the needs of the mongoloids.

We watched Eliza dance awhile longer, but it wasn't anything I hadn't seen before—nor Cage, judging by his nonplussed expression—so I said, "So what can I do for you, Mr. Cage?"

Then, in one of the proudest moments of my life, he said, "Call me Nic," and raised his glass to me. "Reggie, I'd like to make a sequel to *Damn Dirty Apes.*"

"No shit," I said. "About the Backseat Strangler thing?"

"The Showdown at Harry's Pre-Owned American Auto thing."

"Made the news out in Hollywood, huh?"

"No, I caught it on *America's Dumbest Criminals.*"

"Right . . ."

"I want to buy your story rights, Reggie."

He reached inside his jacket and pulled out a check. I'd never seen so many zeroes before. Apart from my bank balance, that is; except these zeroes had a number *in front* of them.

This was it, a second chance . . .

All right, a third chance.

"There's just one problem," Cage said. "The ending."

"What about it?"

"We don't have one," he said. "The bad guy got away."

"Well, shit, Nic. I tried my best—"

"No one's saying you didn't *try*, Reggie. But a Hollywood movie can't end with the bad guy getting away. It's what we call in the biz—" He made finger quotes in the air, "A *downer*. And while we're on the subject of downers, the dog can't die of a cocaine overdose, either. Or any other thing. That's another rule set in stone."

"So what are you saying here? You want me to catch Mitchell Coogler? 'Cause I'll tell you right now, Nic, I don't know I'm up to that."

Cage chuckled at my naivety. "Of course you're not. No, no, no. We'll just invent a dramatic climax. You remember the showdown between me and Malkovich in *Con Air*?"

"How could I forget?"

"It's not like real life; in Hollywood, a satisfying ending is essential."

I took a chug of Coors and thought about the ending I'd like to see . . .

It starred Sue and me. I'd put a ring on it, and we were living together in a nice little house in a goodish part of town, Sue had a bun in the oven and I was the baker. I'd jacked in my job at The Henhouse, but still drank there weekends, in moderation. With Sue's help, I'd opened my own boxing gym—The Hit Pit—and was giving back to Bigelow the best way I knew: By teaching her children how to roll with the punches that life was gonna throw at them. One of my kids, I called him The Kid, coached him all the way to a title shot. The pinnacle of my boxing career had been fighting Boar Hog Brannon for the state strap at light heavy. 'Course, that had also been my boxing rock bottom, because Boar Hog damn near killed me. But The Kid, with me coaching him, all my years of experience and wisdom, he'd go all the way. And me? Hell, there was still a little life in the old dog yet. I'd have a beef with The Kid's rival's coach. Like Mr. Miyagi and that Cobra Kai cocksucker in *The Karate Kid*. Yeah, that'd be sweet. The kids'd be slugging it out in the prize ring, while the coaches went at it in the parking lot. Do I even have to tell you who'd win? The movie would end with a rousing freeze frame of The Kid and me with our arms raised in victory while a power ballad wailed on the soundtrack . . . It sounded like a surefire hit to me.

But before I could pitch my preferred happy ending to Cage, another ending presented itself, as written by the devil his ownself.

3.

After faking his suicide at Beetner's Leap, Mitchell Coogler had not, as Gooch and the law believed, skipped town and sought sanctuary among his neo-Nazi brethren. With Coogler's dreams of a new life with Billy/Billie reduced to ashes along with Harry's car dealership, perhaps he actually *had* contemplated hurling himself to his death from the bluff? But, no . . .

Instead he had fled into the vast sprawl of woods beyond town, the Sticks. There, like a fairytale ogre, he'd taken refuge in a cave. Digging Shelby's bullet from his shoulder, he'd cleaned and dressed the wound, foraged the forest for food and water, and slowly nursed himself back to health. And all the while there was only one thought burning in his brain . . . *Revenge.*

One morning, Coogler was awoken by gunfire, and drunken laughter, echoing over the Sticks. Fearing, at first, that the law had discovered him, he stealthily investigated the noise, and spied a pair of yokel yahoos, Eddie 'Clusterfuck' Clutterbuck and Toby Muntz—Henhouse regulars, you bet—out there blasting squirrels with Eddie's new toy: A fully automatic M4 assault rifle. About the only thing missing was the mounted grenade launcher. Even Coogler thought it was overkill for squirrel.

But it was perfect for the big game he planned on hunting. This was the opportunity he'd been waiting for. Almost like Billy-boy was sending him a sign from up in heaven.

Biding his time until Eddie was reloading the rifle, Coogler blitzed the drunken oafs with a tree branch, bashing their skulls until what passed for their brains was leaking from their ears. He requisitioned the rifle, plus the dozen mags of ammo in Eddie's combat vest. Then, that very same afternoon, loaded for bouncer, Coogler emerged from the Sticks like a vengeful wraith . . .

And descended on The Henhouse to have his revenge.

4.

There was a thunder of automatic gunfire. The windows exploded in a blizzard of glass. Bullets tore through the room, devouring the furniture like a plague of lead locusts. Walt dove to the floor behind the slab. Bottles shattered above his head like targets at a carnival shooting gallery. Booze rained down over him; he was wearing his Skunk Ape cocktail like a reeking cologne. One of the barflies bolted for the fire door and was scythed down, dancing to Eliza's music in a bloody jitterbug of death. The guy's buddies hit the deck, ducking and covering like they were in an old A-bomb infomercial. Eliza leapt down from the stage. Bullets pinged off the dance-pole with flashes of sparks. She cowered beneath Lou's table with Lou and Marlene. Marlene took up most of the room, but her bulk provided an ample body shield for Lou and Eliza.

Bullets ripping the room apart, I dragged Cage from the booth, pulled him down behind the pinball machine, and we took cover.

Walt shouted at me from his foxhole behind the bar slab, "Kinda wish I had my shotgun!"

"Get everyone out back!"

"The hell with that, I ain't moving!"

"Eliza! Get everyone out back!"

Shamed into action, Walt fetched the fire extinguisher from behind the bar. He smashed the nozzle against the floor. Fire retardant billowed from the cylinder like steam from a pipe. He lobbed the fire extinguisher over the slab, and it skated across the room, fogging the bar with fire retardant, and creating a smokescreen for Eliza and the others to flee.

"You're good to go!"

Eliza rallied the regulars and started leading them in a hands-and-knees conga line towards the fire door. Lou couldn't believe his luck, wedged between Eliza and Marlene, Eliza's ass in his face, Marlene's nose up his butt; he'd die a happy man, if it came to that.

The fire exit was blocked from outside. The dumpster had been shoved against the door to block any escape. Eliza's frantic message traveled back along the Human Centipede: "We're trapped in here!"

There was a lull in the shooting as the gunman reloaded.

Then a familiar voice called out, "Levine! Reggie Levine!"

Feeling like a contestant on *The Price is Right*, I peeked above the parapet of the pinball machine. I squinted through the haze of cordite and fire retardant.

Out in the parking lot, Cage's chopper pilot was cowering on his knees before Coogler, who held the muzzle of the assault rifle to the back of his skull.

"Niccy!" the pilot yelled. "Help me, bro!"

Coogler clubbed the man silent with the butt of his rifle.

Cage—God love him—started rising from behind the pinball machine to help his friend. I pushed him back down. "No," I said. "You're too important." I'll admit I was also thinking about the check he'd given me, if I ever lived to cash it.

Coogler saw me peeking above the pinball machine.

"Get your ass out here, Levine. Me n' you got unfinished business."

I hesitated; hell, I put down roots.

"You make me come in there and fetch you out," Coogler said. "Everyone dies."

Walt said, "Better do what he says, Reggie." I'd like to think he was considering the safety of his patrons, and not just his own ass.

I looked at Cage and said, "How's the hero going out in a blaze of glory work for an ending?" I took a deep breath and then forced myself up from behind the pinball machine, projecting an aura of fearlessness that must've been about as convincing as Cage's hair. I squared my shoulders, sucked in my gut. Broken glass crunched beneath my boots as I strode through the bar.

I glanced at Walt, Eliza, Lou and Marlene, silently saying my final farewells. Walt was stoic. Eliza's eyes glistened with tears. Lou crossed himself. All I could see of Marlene was her big chunky butt sticking out from under the table.

I stepped outside through the shattered glass doors.

The smoke ghosted away to reveal Coogler.

Life as a fugitive had token its toll. He'd lost a good dozen pounds, shrinking from superheavy- to plain heavyweight. His face was haggard, his cheeks bearded; his circus strongman mustache was ragged and drooped like a Mexican bandito's. His shaved scalp had grown out into a frizzy 'fro that might've raised eyebrows among his Brotherhood brothers. His clothes were filthy and he clearly hadn't bathed since he'd gone on the lam. The smell of him, he could've passed for the Bigelow Skunk Ape . . . only armed with an assault rifle.

"Good to see you, Reggie."

"Wish I could say the same, Coogler."

Coogler dragged the pilot to his feet. "Get this bird started." The pilot climbed unsteadily into the cockpit. The engine roared. The rotors started turning. Coogler grinned at me. "Come fly with me, Reggie. Let's fly, let's fly away."

I shot an anxious glance at the chopper.

"We couldn't do this from down here? I ain't much for heights." Hot air ballooning above a burning car dealership had done little to cure my phobia.

"How are you about being knee-capped?"

He fired a few shots at my feet and I did a terrified moonwalk and said, "Let's go for a ride, sure, why not."

Coogler herded me into the back of the bird, the rifle barrel jammed into my spine. The passenger cabin was plusher than my apartment. Coogler and me sat facing each other on white leather seats, me with my back to the pilot, Coogler with his gun leveled at me. "Take her up," Coogler barked at the pilot.

The chopper lifted off the ground and began a slow vertical ascent. The pilot was clearly stalling for time. For all the good it did me; I couldn't see a way out of this. The best I could hope for was that Coogler killed me quick.

I said, "Where we going?"

"On our honeymoon."

I must've misheard him over the rotor noise. "Say—say what?"

"You ain't much my type," he said. "Not as pretty as my Billy-boy."

"Sorry to hear it. But, hey. Plenty more fish in the sea—"

"But you'll do in a pinch. 'Course, we'll have to operate first. Get rid of your pecker and those big brass balls of yours. And there ain't no money for no surgeon no more—you saw to that—so I'll just do the best I can with a knife."

He leered at me. "You ever been someone's woman, Reggie?"

My heart started thumping and I swallowed hard. Being de-dicked was gonna seriously hamper things with Sue and me. "Now wait a minute—"

"What's the problem, Levine?" He reached across the cabin, grabbed one of my man-tits and twisted it hard. "Hell, you're half the way there already."

I yelped and slapped his hand away and crossed my arms across my chest self-consciously. "Castrating me isn't gonna bring Billy back!" Not something I ever expected to hear myself saying.

Coogler bashed the rifle stock into my wounded thigh. My stitches split like shirt seams and I roared in pain, clutching my thigh. Blood soaked through the bandages, and the leg of my pants. "Don't you dare say his name!"

From the corner of my eye, I clocked Walt and Cage scurry from the smoking ruins of The Henhouse, and take cover behind my new Wideside.

Of all the trucks, in all the parking lot, they just *had* to choose mine.

Walt watched Cage's back as Cage unspooled the steel cable from the truck winch. I hoped like hell they weren't planning what I thought they were.

Coogler caught my anxious gaze and glanced down from the chopper.

"Is—is that *Nicolas Cage?*"

I told him it was indeed.

He shook his head, as if he'd thought today was fresh out of surprises.

Then he sprayed a rifle burst down at Cage. "I hate your fucking movies!"

Coogler truly was a monster.

Cage and Walt ducked for cover behind my truck. Bullets Swiss-cheesed the doors and shattered the windows. The hood cover tore away and went flipping through the air; it looked as if the painted pterodactyl was taking flight. The tires burst like balloons and the truck sagged to one side with a dying sigh of air.

I felt emasculated, even before Coogler took my cock and balls.

5.

As the chopper continued its slow vertical ascent . . .

Cage finished unspooling the cable from the winch.

The steel hook at the end of the cable was like a grappling hook.

"You really think this'll work?" Cage said.

"Nope," Walt said. "In fact, I'm pretty sure it won't. But Reggie's gotta know we tried."

Cage twirled the cable above his head like a cumbersome lasso. Before the chopper could climb too high, he released the cable and let it fly. It snaked through the air and the hook snagged onto one of the skids with a metallic clang.

Walt and Cage exchanged a glance of surprise.

"How 'bout that," Walt said.

Then he hit the brake on the winch.

The cable snapped taut, yanking the chopper like a kite on a string.

6.

Coogler was thrown from his seat, tossed across the cabin towards me. I grabbed the rifle barrel and twisted it away. He fired off a shot, deafening in the enclosed space of the cabin, and I screamed as the red-hot barrel branded my palm. The bullet ripped past my head, punched a hole through my seat, the pilot's seat behind it, the pilot's back and chest, and finally the windshield. Blood spattered the Plexiglas. Cold air devilled inside through the bullet hole. The pilot gave a grunt and slumped over the controls. The chopper went into a wild tailspin, engine squealing as it spiraled sickeningly towards earth—

7.

I gasped back to consciousness, tweezed my eyes open, and found myself sprawled in the parking lot. The crash must have hurled me from the cabin. I'd blacked out for a second or two, or I'd died, and hell was The Henhouse, which I wasn't ruling out. I looked around, but couldn't see Coogler anywhere. With a little luck—lord knows I was due some—he'd died in the crash, and died hard.

I squinted to see through the thick black smoke billowing from the wreckage of the chopper and—

My truck . . .

The chopper had landed on the roof of my truck, pancaked it flat. The Wideside was wearing the whirlybird like a rakishly angled hat, the still-roaring rotor the hat's razor-sharp brim.

Well, I knew how *this* went; next the fucking thing would explode.

Before that happened, I started bellying away from the wreck—

Something roared behind me.

I glanced back and cried out in horror.

A bloody-beaked pterodactyl was swooping down at me from the sky.

I rolled on my back and shielded my face with my arms.

The pterodactyl smashed against my forearms with a metallic clang.

Coogler was alive and well. Clutching my truck's ripped-off, shot-up hood cover. Clobbering me with the sheet of metal like a Heel wrestler bludgeoning a Baby Face with a folding chair. As he clubbed me with the hood cover, all I could see was that damned pterodactyl, swooping down at me, again and again, like a Harryhausen stop-motion monster. As I raised my arms to defend myself, the beast's beak really *was* bloody now, my crimson handprints smearing the hood cover.

Coogler hefted the metal to land another crunching blow.

I lashed at his knee with the heel of my boot.

Coogler roared in pain, and hobbled back, dropping the hood cover to clutch at his knee, the metal crashing to the ground like a club comic's cymbal. I staggered to my feet, my wounded leg screaming in protest, my thigh soaked with blood where the stitches had split. I put up my dukes and beckoned Coogler in.

But Coogler didn't fight by Queensbury rules.

He charged me like a bull, ducking under my punches, wrestling me into a tight embrace. He locked his forearms around the small of my back, clutched his wrist with his other hand, and *squeeeeezed* me like a nut in a nutcracker. The breath fled my lungs in an agonized wheeze. He tightened his grip, hoisting my feet off the ground. I heard the cartilage in my spine popping like bubblewrap. I flailed my arms and slapped at him pitifully. He laughed in my face. I smelled his rank breath. The lucky sonofabitch: Breathing.

"That's it, Reggie!" I heard Walt cheer. "You got him, son!"

Like I was holding my own, and not being slowly crushed to death.

8.

Walt and Cage had scrambled to the downed chopper and were trying to free the wounded pilot from the cockpit. The cockpit door had buckled when the chopper crashed. Walt and Cage were wrenching at the warped metal like starving men at a sardine tin. Inch by inch, they levered the door open.

The rotor roared above their heads, buffeting their clothes, and Cage's hairpiece, the tails of his mullet flailing wildly in the windstorm—

Then the toupee tore free from his pate with a sound like Velcro.

The rug soared towards me like a magic carpet.

I stuck out my arm and snatched it triumphantly from the air.

Coogler's eyes widened in shock.

With a wheezing battle cry, I whipped the length of the mullet around his neck. Had Cage been wearing a more conservative hairpiece, I would've been a dead man for sure. With the last of my strength, I wrenched the mane of synthetic hair tighter around Coogler's throat—just like my old sparring partner, the Backseat Strangler had taught me. Now it was a war of attrition; could Coogler suffocate me, or snap my spine . . . or would I garrote him first with Nicolas Cage's hairpiece?

Coogler's face flushed red. He started hacking for breath like a dog choking on a chicken bone. Spittle sprayed from his bluing lips, spattering my face. But this was a death match, and he kept crushing the life from me with every last ounce of his hate.

I couldn't feel my legs anymore. My head felt fit to burst like a zit. Darkness clouded the edges of my vision. The blood roared in my ears even louder than the chopper rotor.

Still squeezing me to death, even as he was choking, Coogler started staggering towards the chopper's roaring rotor. He meant to hurl me into the blades. Juice me like fruit in a blender. I pulled tighter on the ends of my makeshift garrote. The synthetic hair was beginning to fray like old rope. It looked like it would snap at any moment.

Then Coogler's death grip suddenly relaxed around the small of my back.

For one horrifying moment, I thought he'd hurled me at the rotor.

I felt myself falling . . . slipping down through the slackening ring of Coogler's arms . . . and then I dropped to the ground like a linebacker at the scrimmage.

I took a quick breath—

Coogler clutched at his throat and sucked a great gulp of air—

I hoped he enjoyed it; it was his last breath.

I sprang up and slugged him with a left hook to the gut. He folded like a deck chair. I jacked an uppercut under his jaw that hurled him back through the air . . . and straight into the threshing teeth of the rotor blade. It was like a magic trick; one minute he was there, the next he wasn't. POOF! And he was gone. Except it was a sight more grisly than just POOF! There was a sound like a wood chipper grinding a log, an ear-splitting shriek, and Coogler vanished in a violent red spray. Viscera drenched me like I was front-row for Shamu at SeaWorld. Coogler's death's head belt buckle skittered to the ground like a hubcap thrown from an auto wreck. Then there was a pop and flash of sparks as the chopper's engine finally crapped out. The rotors slowed to a creaking stop. Chunks of dripping meat clung to the blades like a cannibal shish kebab. A literal red mist drizzled down over the parking lot.

I glanced across the lot and saw Walt and Cage, with the rescued chopper pilot's arms slung around their shoulders, all of them gaping at me in horror.

"Holy . . . fucking . . . shit . . ." someone said.

Might've been Walt.

Might've been Cage.

Hell, it might've been me; I'd gone a little blood simple.

Eliza, Marlene, Lou, and the other survivors, emerged from the ruins of The Henhouse.

Everyone staring at me; no one saying a word.

I stood there staring back at them, teetering for balance, still clutching Cage's hairpiece like an Injun with a freshly peeled scalp. I was covered in Coogler from head to toe. Globs of gore slopped on the asphalt like I was sweating red jellyfish. Mopping the blood from my wild eyes, I turned towards Cage and I dredged up my voice, and I croaked:

"THE END."

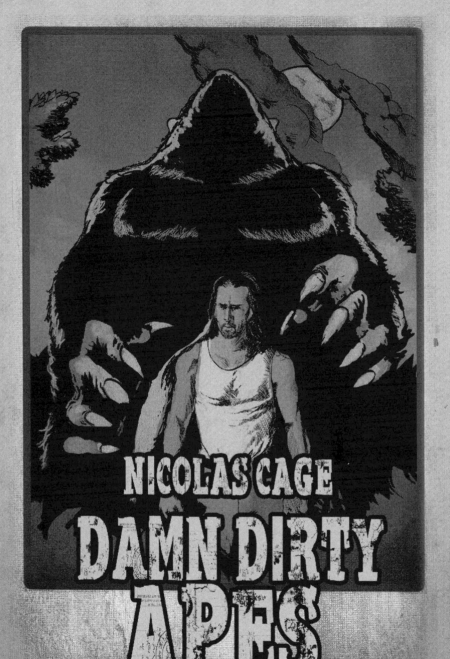

STORY NOTES

A few readers have told me they enjoy reading my story notes.

The rest of you have remained utterly silent on the matter; I can only assume you consider these stories behind the stories to be self-indulgent blather. Rest assured, you can safely close this book without missing anything. Thanks for coming, and don't let the cover hit you on the ass on your way out.

OK, they're gone; let's talk about them . . .

I had a helluva time writing the first Reggie Levine misadventure, *Damn Dirty Apes,* thought the character had legs, and decided to revisit that world.

I'd be lying if I said there was any real method behind the madness of *Tijuana Donkey Showdown,* but these are some of the elements that inspired me . . .

I started with the idea of an actual mule being used to mule drugs. But, me being me, a mere mule wasn't gonna cut it. So I made my mule an adult entertainment animal, and the star of a Mexican 'donkey show.'

How far did I take my research? I hear you ask. Did I actually witness a live donkey show in preparation for this book, in order to give my readers the gritty realism they have come to expect from the author of titles like *Jesus In A Dog's Ass* and *Of Badgers*

& Porn Dwarfs? Alas, I was unable to attend a live donkey show; although Gabino Iglesias assures me the offer remains open when I next visit the States. However, in the name of art, I did investigate this particular paraphilia at notorious bestiality website, *Rustler*. (The site has since been shut down pending the outcome of a lawsuit issued by Larry Flynt; curious parties should contact me personally for the video(s).) Rest assured, I was thorough in my research . . . And that it was not my proudest wank.

For Coogler and Billy's drug-smuggling scheme, I solicited the advice of my local veterinarian. (That was an interesting conversation. Initially, I think he thought I was proposing an actual drug deal.) To my surprise, he agreed that it would be possible for a donkey to mule narcotics, and for the drugs to later be removed as described in the book—on a strip club pool table, with whiskey used as anesthetic—and for the animal to survive the operation. Admittedly, I took rather more poetic license than the fine details he described, and I would advise drug traffickers (a large part of my readership, I am told) to consider other means than a jackass for smuggling your product.

The inspiration for Randy-Ray Gooch's allergic reaction came from a documentary I saw about counterfeit laundry detergent dealers, also known as 'bucket sellers.' It was a fly on the wall documentary in which we followed an overzealous Anti-Counterfeit

Agent (think David Brent with a badge and gun) as he busted a dirt-poor bucket seller brewing bootleg Tide in his garage to sell at swap meets. This was a full-blown arrest involving *hut-hut-hut* SWAT team, K-9 unit, choppers, you name it—Seal Team 6 didn't have such resources when they took down Bin Laden—all to collar this one poor schmuck. Playing up to the cameras, the Agent in Charge started giving the bucket seller a hard time. Like the guy was a heroin pusher selling dope to school kids. "You ever seen the rashes this stuff gives people!" He reminded me of Frank Oz in the movie *Trading Places:* "Angel dust! You ever see what this stuff does to kids!" The entire operation was so overblown, and peculiarly American, that I found it hilarious, and it eventually found its way into the book.

We need to talk about Nicolas . . . I should state for the record that I am a great admirer of Mr. Cage. It's a travesty that for today's younger viewers, Cage is perhaps better known as an internet meme, than for his sterling acting work. Today his truly great films are few and far between, but Cage himself always gives his all to every role. I struggle to think of a single film in which Cage phones in his performance, even when the film is clearly beneath his talents.

Within the world of the story, it seemed perfectly plausible that Nicolas Cage would play Reggie Levine in the movie adaptation of *Damn Dirty Apes*. Needless to say, this would not be one of Cage's prestige pictures, but rather a shoddy Video on Demand affair, with a bad CGI skunk ape, most likely directed by Uwe Boll. This is not, I hasten to add, how I myself would wish to see a *Damn Dirty Apes* movie produced. (For what it's worth, I always pictured Danny Mc-Bride as Reggie . . . with Nicolas Cage playing great white skunk ape hunter, Jameson T. Salisbury.) But within the world of the story, I reckon this is how things would've panned out for poor Reggie; that the film of his life would be trashed by the critics, and sweep the board at the Razzies.

Side-note: I once worked on a screenplay which, last I heard, the producer had earmarked for Nicolas Cage. As of this writing, nothing has come of the project. But should it ever see the light of day, I suspect it will be the kind of movie of which Nicolas Cage memes are made.

CLEAN-UP
ON AISLE 3

Donnie sat in his beat-to-shit Pinto with the heater on full, huddling for warmth beneath the driver's-side window that wouldn't quite shut. An icy wind whipped through the half-inch gap, numbing his hands as he checked the .38 Special. He shoved the piece in his coat pocket, and then stared across the street at the mini mart, the neon KWIK STOP sign flashing red and blue in the night. It was the only store on the downtown strip still open this late. All the other stores had their shutters lowered, tagged with graffiti like tribal markings. Through the window he saw the scrawny Arab storekeeper perched behind the counter reading a magazine. Donnie hadn't seen any customers since he pulled up outside. The guy was alone in there. Just him and the cash register.

Checking his reflection in the rearview, Donnie gave a pained sigh. He looked and felt like stepped-on shit, sick with whatever bug was going around. Last thing he needed was to be pulling a job. But he was already late on this week's vig. He didn't pay what he owed and the flu would be the least of his problems.

He reached across the car to pop the glove compartment, fished out his lucky ski mask. Black wool, trimmed with red around the eyes and mouth. Dusting off the mask, he yanked it down over his head and then rolled it back up in a beanie hat. Donnie honked his nose into a snot rag, stuffed the hanky in his pocket with the piece, pumped himself up with a few wheezy breaths, and then he clambered from the Pinto and started crossing the street to the KWIK STOP.

The bell above the door tinkled as he entered. The cramped little store was divided into three narrow aisles, the shelves stockpiled like a doomsday prepper's bunker. Loud ethnic music was playing: trumpets and drums and off-key warbling like a cat being castrated. The storekeeper glanced up from his magazine. Leathery olive skin and a gray goatee beard, his bald pate polished to a gleaming shine. He wore a white collarless shirt and a ratty old cardigan. The guy reminded Donnie of the limey actor who went blackface to play Gandhi.

On the counter beside him a *No Checks, No Credit* sign was taped to the back of the register. Donnie cut a glance at the security camera above the cigarette rack. The very latest model . . . from the 90s. If the damn thing even worked, the playback would be a blizzard of static. It was probably just for show, to scare off amateurs.

Not taking any chances, Donnie bowed his head

and shielded his mug from the camera's gaze as he sloped to the beer cooler opposite the counter. At the front of the store was a discount DVD bin, and a half-price arsenal of fireworks for New Years, the boxes all stacked in a pyramid like one giant rocket. Donnie glanced down the three aisles for customers or other employees. He didn't see anyone. Just a lonely-looking mop and bucket in Aisle 2. The storekeeper was clearly no neat freak; the shelves were dusty, the goods caked in grime. The place could've used a good airing. It reeked worse than Donnie's fleapit apartment, and that was smelling something. At the back of the store was the liquor display, a few ragged cobwebs clinging to the bottles, and a steel door marked STAFF ONLY. Donnie couldn't hear anything behind the door, but it was hard to tell over the blaring music. Maybe the storekeeper lived back there with his wife and their litter of kids? *The hell with it.* He'd be gone before anyone even knew it.

With his back to the storekeeper, Donnie tugged his lucky ski mask down over his face and then reeled towards the counter, whipping the .38 from his pocket.

"Okay, asshole!" he shouted above the music. "You know what this is!"

The storekeeper glanced up from his magazine as if Donnie had only asked him to price check an item. Seeing the revolver in Donnie's fist, the man's dark eyes narrowed. He rose slowly from his stool, raising his hands. Unlike Donnie's they were steady as a rock. The guy looked so calm, Donnie wondered if he even spoke English.

Then he said, with a heavy accent: "Oh yes, my friend, I know what *this* is."

"Just open the register and gimme the money, you won't get hurt."

The storekeeper gave a curt nod, well versed in armed robbery etiquette.

Lowering one hand, he reached slowly towards the cash register and pressed a button—

And suddenly he wasn't there.

Donnie blinked in surprise.

The fucking guy just disappeared.

Peering over the counter, Donnie saw a trapdoor—the door still swinging where the storekeeper had dropped down into the basement onto a mattress. Splayed out on his back, the man glared up at Donnie with a hateful grin. Then he slashed a finger across his throat, before rolling off the mattress and out of sight.

"The fuck?" Donnie muttered—

And then steel shutters crashed down over the front door and window. The power went out, the store went black, and the music and even the hum of the refrigerators shut off, entombing the place in sudden silence.

It took a moment for Donnie's eyes to adjust to the gloom. He rolled his ski mask back up into a beanie. Stood gaping at the shutters in disbelief.

He'd never seen shutters *inside* a store before. He banged his fist against the shutters—thick steel, like the treads of a tank. Donnie lashed out with his boot until his knee buckled, and he hobbled back in pain. Feeling his skin crawl, he glanced up at the winking red eye of the security camera above the cigarette rack, shuddering as he pictured the storekeeper silently watching him.

He scurried behind the counter, ignoring the register, the cash now forgotten. Careful not to fall through the open trap, Donnie searched beneath the counter for a button or something to raise the shutters. What the hell had the storekeeper pressed to drop the trapdoor? Donnie couldn't even find a panic button. And now that he thought of it, why wasn't any alarm sounding?

Crouching warily above the open trap, he peered down into the dingy basement. All he could see was the mattress where the storekeeper had landed. "Hey!" Donnie shouted down, panic in his voice. "Open these fucking shutters!"

He could hear the storekeeper cursing in Arabic, like a camel clearing phlegm from its throat. The guy sounded pissed, like this wasn't the first time his store had been held up, but by Allah, it would be the last. Then came the unmistakable *shick-shuck* of a pump shotgun being racked. Donnie darted back from the open trap.

That's why there wasn't any alarm.

The guy planned to take care of business himself.

Donnie looked despairingly at his .38. He never worked with a loaded gun. If the threat of being shot wasn't enough, then the job wasn't worth it. Better to walk away, find some other place to stick up. Ideally with an owner who had enough sense to do what they were told when you stuck a gun in their face.

Until now, he'd thought he was being smart.

Shoving the *useless fucking gun* back in his coat, Donnie scuttled down the aisles towards the STAFF ONLY door at the back of the store. If it was locked, he was screwed. He'd have to take his licks and beg the storekeeper not to kill him. He was almost at the door when he heard the jangle of keys on the other side.

Donnie dove into Aisle 1 and crouched low behind the shelves, cloaking himself in the shadows as the door clattered open. The storekeeper emerged from the back room, clutching a shotgun bigger than he was. He paused to yank the door shut behind him, locking it from a key hoop clipped to his belt.

There was something funny-looking about him. In the gloom, it was hard to tell exactly what. Then the storekeeper turned his head, and Donnie thought he'd lost his mind. A giant frog was sweeping the shotgun left to right across the aisles. Donnie tried to blink away the nightmare. Then he realized the storekeeper was wearing some kind of mask. No . . . Not a mask. Night-vision goggles, the lenses protruding from his head like bulbous amphibian eyes.

Tiny jewels of sweat glittered on the Arab's scalp. He began to sidestep slowly along the end of the aisles, his cheap leather shoes squeaking as he crabbed along—the shotgun steady in his hands as he moved methodically towards Aisle 1—towards Donnie, crouching in the shadows.

Panicking, Donnie snatched a jar of coffee from the shelf in front of him, and then lobbed it over the aisles like a grenade. Glass shattered as it exploded on the far side of the store. The storekeeper pivoted with a squeal of his squeaky shoes. The shotgun roared, the blast punching a hole through the aisles and scattering stock, the deafening noise drowning out Donnie's scream.

This guy wasn't fucking around. He wasn't going to rough him up or make a citizen's arrest. Donnie wasn't talking his way out of this shit. There'd been no hesitation as the storekeeper turned and fired. That blast was intended to cut him in half. The man meant to kill him.

This should've been a quick dollar stickup. Donnie wasn't going to play cat-and-mouse with a shotgun-toting maniac. Let the cops deal with the crazy bastard. He'd take the arrest if it meant he left the KWIK STOP alive.

He dug in his coat for his cellphone. No signal bars on the display. He waved the phone about frantically, searching for a signal. Had the shutters caused some kind of blackout? He raised the phone towards the ceiling. A single signal bar flickered weakly. He listened out for the storekeeper. On the far side of the store, he heard Arabic cursing as the man found the shattered coffee jar and realized he'd been duped. The storekeeper racked the shotgun and started back along the aisles, his shoes squeaking urgently.

Donnie monkeyed up the shelves in front of him. The flimsy wooden shelving boards sagged beneath his weight. His ears were still ringing from the shotgun blast. He could only hope that the storekeeper had also been deafened; that the guy didn't hear him as Donnie slid on top of the shelving unit, disturbing a thick layer of dust that swirled around him in a cloud that prickled his fluey nose.

The storekeeper sprang into the aisle directly below him. When he saw the aisle was empty, the Arab muttered a curse, lowering the shotgun, and then adjusted the sweaty strap of his night-goggles. He was breathing hard. Maybe even excited. Enjoying the thrill of the hunt. He started stalking down the aisle towards the front of the store.

Flattened on top of the shelving unit, Donnie didn't dare move, holding his breath and fighting an almost overwhelming urge to sneeze. From the corner of his eye, he watched as the storekeeper crept along the aisle below him. The man left his line of sight, but Donnie was still able to track him by his squeaky shoe.

He checked his cellphone again, and gave a silent prayer of thanks when he saw there were now *two* signal bars on the display. But before he could dial 911, he inhaled another thick cloud of dust that set his nose ablaze—

The sneeze echoed through the store like a karate cry.

The Arab turned and fired without hesitation, the shotgun belching fire.

Donnie sprang from the shelving unit, shredded cereal boxes exploding behind him, a shower of Kellogg's raining over the store. Slamming into the next shelving unit, he crashed down into Aisle 2, landing heavily on his back next to the mop-bucket, his cellphone shattering on the floor beside him.

The storekeeper racked his shotgun and charged up the aisle towards him. Woofing for breath, Donnie could only flail his legs, kicking over the mop-bucket. Sludgy gray water spewed across the floor. The storekeeper slid on the muck like an Arabic Chevy Chase. He thudded to the floor and fired another deafening blast, plaster raining down from the ceiling.

Before the man could recover, Donnie scrambled to the nearest shelving unit. He slithered across the bottom shelf, clawing through a crinkling wall of potato chip bags, emerging into Aisle 3. Bracing himself against a deep-freeze refrigerator chest, he hauled himself up onto rubbery legs, sucking for breath.

Through the gaps in the shelves, he could see the storekeeper in the center aisle, wobbling to his feet like a prizefighter trying to beat the ref's count.

Racking the shotgun with a grunt, the Arab began limping around the aisle after Donnie, careful not to slip on the sludge-slick floor, one hand clutching at the shelves for balance.

Donnie was still slumped against the deep-freeze, trying to catch his breath. The small of his back was screaming with pain where he'd landed on it. His legs could barely support him, let alone carry him away. Before the storekeeper rounded the aisles and spotted him, Donnie hauled up the lid of the deep-freeze.

Hardly thinking about what he was doing, he slid inside the chest and buried himself among the frozen food packages. As he cowered inside the icy coffin, peering up in terror through the frosted glass, listening to the storekeeper's shoes squeak closer, it occurred to Donnie that as far as dumb fucking ideas went, this was right up there alongside robbing a store with an unloaded gun.

The storekeeper paused next to the deep-freeze. Wheezing for breath, he steadied himself against the refrigerator chest. Donnie stifled a scream as a hand thudded down on the glass lid. For a moment it seemed like the man was staring right down at him. Then he dragged his hand from the glass to wipe the sweat off his forehead. Frowning, the Arab glanced back down the aisle, maybe fearing his prey had circled behind him. Then he moved on to the back of the store.

Donnie waited until he heard the distant jangle of keys as the storekeeper checked whether the STAFF ONLY door was locked. Then he palmed up the glass door of the deep-freeze, and eased himself out, crouching down beside the refrigerator and listening intently. It sounded like the guy was doing another lap of the store.

This time, Donnie would be waiting for the crazy fuck.

He scuttled to the liquor display at the back of the store. Forced to squint in the gloom, Donnie scanned the shelves for firewater, saw a picture of Speedy Gonzales on a dusty label, and grabbed the bottle of *Arriba* 100-proof tequila.

Nodding to himself, he crouched behind the Aisle 2 end-shelf, and then peeked around the corner, waiting for the storekeeper to appear at the front of the store. He unscrewed the bottle cap, wincing at the screech of twisted metal. But the storekeeper didn't seem to hear. Donnie listened to the guy's shoes squeaking as he continued his patrol of the store. Donnie necked a big swig from the bottle. For what he needed to do, and for courage. He shuddered as the tequila burned through him. Snatching his snot rag from his pocket, he began stuffing it into the bottleneck until only a little cloth tongue poked out. Then he pulled his Zippo lighter from his pocket and thumbed the wheel. *Click!*

The storekeeper's shoes stopped in mid-squeak.

The Zippo shook in Donnie's hand as he torched the snot rag fuse.

The shotgun roared. A tower of Heinz cans exploded on the shelf above Donnie's head. Spaghetti sauce sprayed down over him, nearly snuffing out the flame. The storekeeper reloaded, feeding shells into the shotgun like a degenerate gambler playing the slots. Donnie mopped the spaghetti sauce from his eyes and then leapt out from cover. They faced each other like Old West gunfighters. A tin of beans rolled like tumbleweed across the aisle between them. The storekeeper saw the Molotov cocktail in Donnie's hands. His mouth dropped open in shock. He started raising the shotgun.

Donnie Hail Mary-ed the burning bottle . . .

And then he watched in horror as it sailed harmlessly over the storekeeper's head.

The bottle shattered against the steel shutters behind him and burst into flames. The storekeeper stood silhouetted before a wall of fire like a frogheaded demon from hell. Oblivious to the danger behind him, the storekeeper sneered at Donnie as he aimed the shotgun, his finger teasing the trigger—as flames started licking the fireworks display.

There was a blinding white flash and then the

fireworks boomed like Hiroshima. Instantly, the store-keeper became a human fireball, the blast blowing him off his feet and hurling him up the aisles like a missile. He sailed straight past Donnie and crashed into the STAFF ONLY door, thudding to the floor like a piece of barbecue you toss to the dog.

The front of the store was now an inferno. Rockets ignited and screeched from the flames, setting shelves ablaze, the sound deafening inside the steel-shuttered store. The place was fast becoming a death trap.

Donnie crouched beside the charred storekeeper. He took off his coat and smothered the flames of the man's burning cardigan. Wrestling the key hoop from his belt, Donnie juggled the red-hot keys, yelping as they scorched his palms. Wrapping his coat around his hand like an oven glove, he unlocked the STAFF ONLY door to reveal another locked door marked DELIVERY, and stairs leading down to the base-ment. Donnie knelt in front of the second door and sorted through the jumble of keys, trying to find the key that would fit the lock—

Something squeaked behind him.

Glancing over his shoulder, he saw the store-keeper staggering to his feet. His face was flame-grilled hamburger. The night-goggles were melted onto his head like devil horns. He propped himself up in the doorway, smoke coiling from the scorched rags of his cardigan. Before Donnie could stand, the Arab lunged at him, slamming the shotgun across his throat, pinning him back against the door. The fire had fused the shotgun to his hands. The melted flesh of his fingers was webbed across the stock as he crushed Donnie's larynx.

Choking, Donnie grappled the shotgun and shoved the guy back. They stumbled across the landing, tumbling down the stone steps and thudding onto the concrete floor of the basement. Landing on top of Donnie, the storekeeper jammed the shotgun back across his throat and pressed down with all his weight. Donnie spluttered and bucked, the key hoop in his hand jangling wildly as he flailed at the man's face before he slammed a long mortise key through the left lens of the Arab's night-goggles, driving it deep into the eye socket. He then wrenched the key in the man's eyeball like he was forcing open a rusty lock.

The storekeeper gave a hog-like squeal. His head jerked back, the keys dangling from his face like bloody jewelry. Yolky yellow gunk gushed from the shattered lens of his goggles, spraying across Donnie's face. Gagging, Donnie hammered the heel of his hand against the key, burying it deeper in the Arab's eye. The storekeeper shrieked, lurching to his feet and staggering blindly about the basement. Donnie scrabbled back across the floor, spitting eyeball fluid and heaving for breath.

The Arab crashed against a stock shelf, cans and jars clattering and smashing on the floor around him. He reached up to remove the keys from his eye, before realizing he couldn't—not with the shotgun welded to his hands. His arms twitched pathetically. Once, twice . . . Then all the fight seemed to drain right out of him. His body sagged, and he slumped down on a camp bed parked against the cinderblock wall, the springs squealing like his squeaky shoes.

Huddled on the bed, the man glowered at Donnie with his one good eye, the other a ruined hollow of red and yellow slime. He slowly raised his left knee. Donnie watched in disbelief as the man planted the sole of his shoe against the length of the shotgun and sucked a few shallow breaths . . . before he flexed his leg and the melted flesh of his palms ripped free from the stock with a sound like Velcro tearing. The shotgun clattered to the floor in front of him, but he was too weak to reach for it.

With raw and bloody hands, the Arab grasped the hoop of keys dangling from his face. Donnie covered his mouth with his hand—nearly begged the guy to stop—but he couldn't look away. The Arab yanked on the key hoop. The key ripped from his eye socket with a wet popping sound. He gave a yelp and fainted dead away, flopping back on the camp bed with the keys clutched tightly in his fist.

Donnie almost fainted himself; his head was spinning as he staggered to his feet. He peeled off his ski mask and covered his nose and mouth to keep from choking on the thick black smoke belching down into the basement through the open trapdoor above them. Fiery ash rained down onto the mattress. It wouldn't be long before the fire spread downstairs. Already the basement was baking like a pizza oven.

He took a wary step towards the storekeeper, eyeing the keys clutched in the man's fist. It looked like the guy was out for the count. All it took was getting burned half to death, blasted into a wall, thrown down a staircase and stabbed in the eye. But Donnie wasn't about to take any chances. This guy was like the fucking Terminator.

He kicked the shotgun beyond the Arab's reach. It skidded across the floor and clanged against the legs of a workbench. Donnie paused when he noticed some kind of photo shrine on the wall above the workbench.

The cluster of photos showed a young woman. The storekeeper's wife, Donnie figured. She was beautiful (even in a burning building, Donnie could appreciate a piece of ass) and very pregnant. Beneath the shrine sat a chunky security monitor—but it wasn't showing the store go up in flames. Instead it was hooked to an old VCR player running a short loop of silent film.

The grainy black and white footage was timecoded in the bottom corner, dated six years ago. It showed the storekeeper's pregnant wife as she stood in terror behind the shop counter. She was opening the cash register for a jittery punk wearing a stocking mask that mashed his features. He was clutching a pistol in a sideways gangsta-grip. The cash drawer slid open. The punk's pistol spat fire. The back of the woman's long hair flailed as her brains splattered the cigarette rack. Bloody cartons of smokes rained from the rack in a waterfall. The woman crumpled to the floor. Leaning over the counter, the punk raided the cash register, pocketing bills as he fled the store.

The footage looped and played again. And again.

Donnie looked at the cushioned chair parked in front of the monitor, the cushion cratered by the weight of the husband, and the weight of the grief pressing down on him. How long had the storekeeper sat here? Hour after hour . . . day after day . . . watching again and again as his pregnant wife was gunned down by a two-bit stickup man. A piece of shit like Donnie.

Before the footage could loop and play again, Donnie switched off the monitor. He saw his reflection in the blank TV screen, and was about to look away in shame, sickened at the sight of himself. Then something in the screen's reflection caught his eye. A sudden movement behind him.

He wheeled around in time to see the storekeeper swinging a fire extinguisher by the hose like a mace-and-chain. The metal butt of the fire extinguisher scythed across his jaw, smashing teeth and bone, and Donnie dropped like he'd been shot, like the storekeeper's wife, out cold before he hit the deck.

*   *   *

When he came to, Donnie found himself facedown on the cracked concrete floor. His ankles and wrists were bound tightly with duct tape, hogtied behind him. He raised his throbbing head weakly off the floor. A rope of congealed blood drooled from his mouth, puddling like black treacle on the concrete. His vision blurred in and out of focus, but he could see he was still in the basement.

The room was fogged with smoke that was starting to clear. The fire upstairs had been extinguished. The storekeeper must have doused the flames while Donnie was unconsciousness. Donnie listened intently for the wail of EMS sirens outside. Surely someone must have reported World War III breaking out in the KWIK STOP. But all he could hear was the sound of someone digging.

A section of the basement's concrete floor had been broken, probably by the sledgehammer propped against the wall, a slab of stone levered up to reveal the dirt below. The storekeeper was using a shovel to dig a hole in the plot of earth, piling up the dirt beside a steel drum with a skull and crossbones symbol and a label marked LYE. The Arab's wounded hands were swathed in bandages. He grimaced in pain as he worked the shovel. Whenever the pain seemed too much to bear, he would glance at the security monitor on the workbench, watching the footage of his dying wife again, and summon the strength to continue digging.

When he was done, he climbed from the hole and loomed over Donnie.

Donnie tried to beg, but his shattered jaw and blood-clogged mouth allowed only a pitiful choked whimper. The Arab planted a foot on him, his shoes giving the last squeak Donnie would ever hear, as he kicked him into the grave.

Donnie landed on his back, his bound arms and legs twisting painfully beneath him with the impact. He watched in helpless terror as the storekeeper began shoveling the dirt over him. The last thing he saw was what looked like another shrine on the wall directly above him. No photos, this time. Donnie thought this one looked less like a shrine than a trophy wall. Nailed to the cinderblocks was a stocking mask, a bandana, and three ski masks, one of them black wool, with red trim around the eyes and mouth, and not so lucky after all.

ACKNOWLEDGEMENTS

Forever and always the biggest thanks must go to my partner, Suzie, who, as you might have guessed, is currently standing behind me with a gun to my head. (She loves me depicting her as a ball-busting shrew. In my defense, it's the only way I can ensure she reads my books. "What have you written about me THIS time?")

Thanks to my regular editor, 'Burro' Bill Chaney. I was tempted to publish his notes on this book. More than once he commented, "Likely the first time such a phrase has been committed to the English language." I'll leave you to imagine which phrases they were.

Randy Chandler & Cheryl Mullenax @ Comet Press helped me bring this book across the finish line. Thanks, guys!

The crazy talented Mike Tenebrae designed my awesome cover and promotional art. I'm almost reluctant to share him with the rest of you writers looking for art . . . But check him out @ www.tenebraestudios.net

Thank you to my blurbers: Pete Kahle, Sean Costello, Ed Kurtz, Jeff Strand, Gabino Iglesias, Scott Adlerberg, Adam Cesare, and Joey Hirsch. Special fist-bump to James Newman for his endorsement, and for writing such a marvelously antagonistic foreword. Appreciate it, fellas.

Big-up Duncan Bradshaw @ EyeCue Productions for the preorder / promo memes.

Extra special thanks to Erin Sweet-Al Mehairi, who worked as my publicist on the recent Die Dog or Eat the Hatchet tour. Erin did an exceptional job, and I can't recommend her highly enough to other writers looking to create buzz for their books. She also introduced me to a great bunch of new friends, including: Andi 'Eagle Eyes' Rawson, Kim Deveroux (and her Horror After Dark homies), Hunter Shea, Angela Crawford, David Spell, and Rich Duncan.

Thanks also: Paul Cook, Lex Liosatos, Mark Milan, Benoit Lelievre, Dave Wahlman, Tom Leins, Frank Errington, Gef Fox, Eric Beetner, Jason Parent, Rowena Hosean, J. David Osborne, and Max Booth III.

The following reprobates have supported me from the get-go: Jed Ayres, Kent Gowran, Adrian Shotbolt, Dave Dubrow, Shane Keene, Nev Murray (special thanks to Nev for hosting the exclusive Tijuana Donkey Showdown cover reveal @ his Confessions of a Reviewer blog), Zachary Walters, Noelle Holten, Sarah Hardy, Dave Barnett, Chris and Rob @ The Slaughtered Bird . . . "I knew him when" —bragging rights for all of you.

Shout-out to my Goodreads pals: Kelly & Mitchell, Shelby, Bill, Melki, Janie, Karl, Susan, Shayne, Still, Carlos, Jess . . . Too many of you fuckers to name individually— my bad to those of you I forgot!

Lastly, thank you to my readers—it still blows my mind I even HAVE readers.

I hope you dug *Tijuana Donkey Showdown*. Reach out and let me know at Facebook, Goodreads, and Twitter @Adam_G_Howe. And please do me a solid and leave a wee Amazon review. Unless you thought the book sucked, in which case kindly keep the information to yourself, or recommend it to an enemy.

Until next time . . .

ABOUT THE AUTHOR

Adam Howe is a British writer of fiction and screenplays. He lives in Greater London with his partner, their daughter, and a hellhound named Gino. Writing as Garrett Addams, his short story "Jumper" was chosen by Stephen King as the winner of the international *On Writing* contest, and published in the paperback/Kindle editions of King's memoir. His fiction has appeared in places like *Nightmare Magazine, Thuglit, Mythic Delirium*, and *Year's Best Hardcore Horror Volume 1*. He is the author of two novella collections, *Die Dog or Eat the Hatchet,* and *Black Cat Mojo*. In the pipeline: the occult thriller *Scapegoat*, a horror/crime collaboration with Adam Cesare, and 80s action epic, *One Tough Bastard*. Stalk him at Facebook, Goodreads, and Twitter @Adam_G_Howe.

Author photo by Mark Milan

die dog
or eat the
HATCHET

3 NOVELLAS BY
ADAM HOWE

BLACK CAT
MOJO

"Howe weaves a deeply stained tapestry of ne'er-do-wells and addicts, schemers and dreamers, gangsters and wannabes—a nihilist's seriocomic wet dream."
—Walt Hicks, HELLNOTES

ADAM HOWE